'I'll get do... ...want me to...

'In my condition...

He raised an eye...

'I could fall off the chair in shock.'

'You've got a warped sense of humour, Alli.' He grinned, then reached into his shirt pocket and brought out a small blue velvet box.

Inside there was a large solitaire diamond, square-cut, exquisite.

'Thank you, Dex. It's a lovely gesture.'

He frowned. 'It's not a gesture. It's a proposal—a sincere, serious proposal.'

'But not as sincere as when you proposed once before, to...Clare?'

'That was a long time ago.'

'You were in love; you still remember what it feels like.'

'I remember the pain of losing her.' He spoke bluntly. 'If that's what love does to you...' He shook his head. 'I never want to feel that loss again.'

Alicia felt the rawness in his words. It shocked her. Was this man simply scared of risking love again?

The idea started a flicker of hope within her. Perhaps if she was patient...

Kathryn Ross was born in Zambia, where her parents happened to live at that time. Educated in Ireland and England, she now lives in a village near Blackpool, Lancashire. Kathryn is a professional beauty therapist, but writing is her first love. As a child she wrote adventure stories, and at thirteen was editor of her school magazine. Happily, ten writing years later, DESIGNED WITH LOVE was accepted by Mills & Boon®. A romantic Sagittarian, she loves travelling to exotic locations.

A MARRIAGE ON PAPER

BY
KATHRYN ROSS

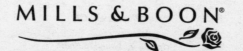

MILLS & BOON®

First published in Great Britain 1999
Harlequin Mills & Boon Limited,
Eton House, 18-24 Paradise Road, Richmond, Surrey TW9 1SR

© Kathryn Ross 1999

ISBN 0 263 81730 X

Set in Times Roman 10½ on 12 pt.
01-9907-51939 C1

Printed and bound in Spain
by Litografía Rosés, S.A., Barcelona

CHAPTER ONE

How was she going to tell him? The question which had wrecked Alicia's sleep for several nights still nagged as she answered the phone.

'Dexter Computer Software,' she said automatically. 'Good morning, how may I help?'

'Hi, Alicia, it's Maddie McDowell here. Put me through to Dex, will you?'

The autocratic crisp tones made Alicia smile. That woman acted as if she owned this business, she thought wryly, but she admired her cool confidence. 'I'll just see if he's available,' she said in equally crisp tones, before flicking the switch through to the inner office.

'Dex, Maddie is on line one. Have you time to speak to her?'

'Of course. Put her through,' was the immediate response. The deep, sexy drawl of her boss's voice brought a shiver to her spine. Hell! she thought as she connected the call. Even the sound of Dex Rowland's voice could turn her on.

She glared at the phone on her desk, as if *it* was responsible for the emotional turmoil eating her up.

It was a long phone call; the red light seemed to be on for ever. Or maybe it was just that time seemed to be dragging this morning.

She glanced at the clock above Dex's door. It was nearly lunchtime. She would wait until he had finished this call, then go in and speak to him. This couldn't be put off any longer.

The light on the telephone went out. This was her chance. She didn't move. Apprehension wouldn't let her. Maybe this was too important to blurt out in the office, she thought frantically. She'd have to find a better time.

'Alicia, can you come in here for a moment, please?' Dex's voice echoing through the intercom made her jump.

Running a smoothing hand down over her simple blue shift dress, she stood up and moved towards the door.

'Hey, great news!' Dex grinned at her. He was leaning back in his leather chair, his hands behind his head, looking relaxed and happy.

Alicia could only look at him and think how attractive he was. Every time she met those dark eyes she felt as if he stole a little bit more of her heart. It was insidious, it was extreme, but it happened each time he looked at her.

He was twenty-seven, and he had the kind of regular, handsome good looks usually found on the movie screen. Dark hair, neatly cut, a face that was strong, a physique that always made women take a second look. Yet somehow he seemed unaware of the power his looks had over the opposite sex; his mind was usually preoccupied with his work.

Did he have any idea just how much she loved him? she wondered, with a twist of her heart.

'Maddie loved my designs.'

'Of course she did,' Alicia said with a smile. 'You're a genius. One day you're going to design a computer program that will make you wealthy beyond your wildest dreams.'

Dex regarded her steadily for a moment. 'I love it when you talk dirty, Alicia Scott,' he drawled with lazy humour. 'Tell me some more.'

'Well...' She put her hands on his leather-topped desk and leaned slightly forward, warming to her theme.

He watched her absently for a moment. Her long blonde hair was drawn back from her face in a ponytail, and she wore no make-up, yet her skin was perfectly clear and fresh, her lips peachy soft, her long lashes naturally dark.

For all that, she wasn't what you would call beautiful in the conventional sense of the word. She was more striking. Back home in America they would have described her as 'preppy', because she certainly had class. There was something about her that captured attention and held it. Perhaps it was the large blue eyes, the high cheekbones…or maybe it was just that she was tall and had a fabulous body which she held ramrod straight.

'Henry Banks and George Mitton are hungry to sign you up…the letters are in your in-tray. Their esteem for your talent is very evident in the fact that they've both rung twice this morning, wanting to know when you'll get back to them.'

Dex grinned. 'Changed days, eh?'

'Certainly are.' There had been a time, not so long ago, when the prestigious firms belonging to Mitton and Banks would have asked, Dex who? Now they were sitting up and paying respectful attention. It was all very promising.

She leaned even further across towards him. 'So, who are you going to choose?'

'Neither.' His eyes moved to the round neck of her dress. He could just see the creamy lace of her bra. It distracted him. 'Madeline McDowell has come up with the most interesting offer.'

'Really?' She straightened. This knowledge disturbed her. Why, she had no idea. This was business…this was Dex's world and he excelled in it. She merely took letters and phone calls and organised his office with brisk efficiency. That was it.

'Do you want me to draft a letter to Mitton and Banks? Politely turn down their offers but keep your options open?'

'Nope.' His eyes moved to the buttons at the top of her dress. He reached out and caught her small wrist in his large hand. 'That's not what I want at all.'

She could hear the sexy innuendo in his voice very clearly as his thumb stroked the soft skin on the underside of her wrist. It was the only contact with her body, and yet she felt as if her whole body suddenly caught fire.

'So, what do you want?' Her voice was shyly hesitant, not at all steady.

He tugged at her hand, compelling her to walk around his desk. At the same time he pushed his chair backwards.

'I think you know,' he murmured.

'This isn't appropriate behaviour for the office.' She tried to sound disapproving, but she made no effort to desist when he pulled her down on to his knee.

'I know,' he admitted huskily. 'But I've told you before not to come to work looking so damned sexy. You're a distraction.'

She looked down at the pale blue shift dress she wore. It wasn't remotely sexy. It stopped at a sensible length, just above her knee, and it skimmed her figure in a way that wasn't even slightly revealing. 'I'm not a distraction at all.'

'Aren't you?' He trailed one finger down the side of her face. The effect was so devastatingly sensual that she felt her body starting to respond to him in a very strong manner.

His finger trailed down her neck and traced the neckline of her dress. It created little shivers of sensation inside her that were deliciously tormenting. 'Then it must be the heady mention of success. That will turn me on every time.'

'I'll have to remember that,' she murmured huskily, and reached to kiss him.

At first her lips were gentle, uncertain, then he took control and the kiss deepened, became fevered with desire. Her fingers raked through the dark thickness of his hair as she pressed herself closer.

She felt him unbuttoning her dress, felt the cool caress of his fingers against her heated flesh. His hand closed over the rounded peak of her breast, brushed it with masterful, erotic strokes until she felt hard darts of wanton passion taking her over completely.

The shrill ring of the telephone interrupted them. 'Damn!' He broke away from her.

She wanted to tell him to leave it. She wanted him to just continue kissing her, caressing her. Wanted everything else to go away.

Their eyes met. 'I...I can't answer it,' she said unsteadily. Her breathing was uneven, her mind chaotic.

He reached out and picked up the receiver from the desk in front.

'Dex speaking.' His voice was crisp, businesslike. Alicia found herself marvelling at his composure. No one could have guessed that two seconds ago he had been as out of control as her. Or had he? She frowned.

'What this afternoon?' he asked, sounding very alert.

His other hand left the rosy, aching hardness of her breast to reach for his desk diary. 'Well, I had a lunch appointment, but it's nothing I can't reschedule for later,' he murmured. 'OK, see you then.'

Alicia started to straighten her clothing. She was buttoning up her dress as he put the phone down.

'Sorry, Alli.'

'That's OK.'

'That was Maddie. She's set up a lunchtime meeting with a banker friend of hers.'

Alicia's eyebrow's rose. 'She works fast!'

'Yes, she's quite a woman.'

The admiration and respect in Dex's voice caused a stir of jealousy to rise inside Alicia. She didn't like the feeling at all and she tried to squash it. 'Just as long as you remember that *I'm* the woman you're having the affair with,' she reminded him with a smile, her voice light.

'There's no chance of my forgetting that,' he murmured warmly. His hand went to her breast. 'You've covered yourself up,' he admonished sternly, rubbing gently over the silkiness of her dress. He smiled with satisfaction as he felt her body hardening instantly beneath his touch. 'How about finishing what we've started here later on tonight?' he suggested gently.

'I think that's a wonderful idea.' Immediately she felt better. 'You know it's our anniversary tonight?'

He looked at her in puzzlement.

'Twelve months since you head-hunted me from MacDales.' She grinned. 'Surely you hadn't forgotten?'

He laughed. 'Sorry, I had. But I do recall that I had to wait a full six months before I got the rest of your body.'

He grinned as he noted that he had embarrassed her. He watched the bright flush of colour under her skin. The misty uncertainty in her eyes reminded him of how young she was; just twenty.

'Trust you to remember that date.' She straightened his tie with tender attention to detail. 'Better get back to work,' she said crisply, and pulled herself away from him.

'We'll continue this discussion later.' He smiled. 'I'll come around to your place about eight, all right?'

She nodded.

'Will you dig last year's accounts out of the file for me, Alli?' he asked as she made her way towards the door. 'I have a feeling I might be needing them soon.'

'Yes.' She closed the door behind her and took a deep, shaking breath. What was she going to do…what the *hell* was she going to do? The question beat inside her. She could have told him when he was kissing her. There was just the two of them here; there couldn't be a better time. Now she had succeeded in putting it off again.

She went across to the filing cabinets and got out the figures Dex had asked for. Then she sat down and tried to concentrate on her work.

Half an hour later Dex emerged from his office. She noted he had put the jacket of his suit on and had combed his hair neatly back into place. 'Will I do?' he asked with a grin as he caught her scrutiny.

'Very impressive,' she answered with a laugh. 'No one would ever guess that I had you all mussed up a little while ago.'

'Good.' He went across to the window and looked down towards the street. 'Maddie's here. I'd better go.'

'Good luck.' She watched as he walked towards the door. 'Dex?'

He looked around at her a trifle impatiently.

'You forgot the figures.' She held the folder out to him.

'Hell. Thanks, Alli. What would I do without you?' He took them from her outstretched hand, flashed her a very attractive smile. 'I probably won't be back this afternoon. You can knock off early if you want. Just make sure the answer machine is on.'

The door closed behind him. Something made Alicia get up and go across to the window.

Despite the fact that the Australian day was at its hottest, Maddie had the top down on her silver Mercedes. Looking directly down at her, Alicia could just see the top of her dark hair, cut in a silky bob, and the fact that she was wearing a bubble-gum-pink dress that showed a provocative glimpse of the tops of her legs. As she watched Dex emerged from the building and got into the car.

Maddie reached across and kissed him on the cheek. They talked for a minute, then as she swung the car out from the kerb he took his jacket off and tossed it on the back seat.

Alicia leaned her forehead against the glass and watched as they disappeared down the busy road. Dex's car was parked at the kerb, further down the street. The sight of it brought a smile to her lips. It was no wonder Maddie had picked Dex up; she wouldn't have liked to be seen in his practical old vehicle. For some reason this made her feel better.

Dex deserved this break. He was the most ambitious man she had ever met, and he had worked extremely hard for success. Had ploughed all profits, all savings into his designs.

She had meant it when she had called him a genius this morning. He was talented and he had a sharp mathematical mind. She was certain that this new computer game he had developed would change his fortunes, open doors for him. And if Maddie held a few keys to those doors then that was great. She was happy for him.

But would he be happy when he discovered that he was going to be a father in a little under seven months' time?

CHAPTER TWO

THE air-conditioning wasn't working in the apartment. Alicia had struggled to fix it for the last hour, but to no avail. The heat was making her feel a bit sick.

'Never mind,' she said brightly to her sister. 'Dex will be here soon and he'll be able to sort it out.'

'I wish he'd hurry,' Victoria moaned. 'I've got a load of homework to do, but in this heat all I want to do is fall asleep.'

Alicia glanced at her watch. It was seven o'clock. Maybe if she phoned Dex he would come over early. She picked up the phone and dialled his number.

There was no answer from his apartment. Where could he be until now? Surely still not discussing business with Maddie?

'I'll get you some iced water,' she said to her sister as she put the phone down. 'Maybe that will help.'

Victoria pulled a face. 'It would be a better help if you knew how to do these formulas.'

'I'll have a look, but maths isn't really my subject.' Alicia went over to the fridge. The cool air that hit her when she opened the door was a relief. She felt like leaving it open and pulling their chairs over to sit in the open doorway.

The apartment was far too small for the two of them. There were two tiny bedrooms, with a bathroom between, and then this kitchen-cum-living room. That was it, but it was all Alicia could afford. She was supporting Victoria through school, and that took all her extra cash.

She glanced over at her sister as she threw her pencil down on the kitchen table. 'This is impossible,' she groaned, raking a hand through her long blonde hair in frustration.

'It can't be that difficult.' Alicia poured their drinks and went to sit next to her. Although there were only three years between them, Alicia acted more like a mother towards Vicky than a sister. It had been that way since Alicia was just nine years of age and their parents had died in a car crash.

From that first night when they had found themselves at Albany House Orphanage she had felt protective and responsible. She had been the one to comfort Vicky, had remained strong and put on a brave face. It had been a first lesson on how to hide her feelings. Thinking about someone else meant you didn't have to concentrate on your own feelings of grief, your own fears. In a way it had helped ease the pain of loss. It had certainly made her grow up quickly.

When Alicia had been old enough to leave Albany House she had taken Vicky with her. Now they were quite happy here in this apartment…usually, anyway, when the air-conditioning was working and Alicia didn't feel quite so nauseous.

They struggled on together with the maths project. It was difficult, and they were both so absorbed in it that Alicia didn't notice how late it was getting. It was almost nine when Dex finally arrived at their door.

'Hi, sorry I'm late.' He reached to kiss her cheek.

'Are you?' She glanced at her watch and her eyebrows rose, but she said nothing.

'God, it's hot in here! What have you done to the air-conditioning?' Dex strolled over to the control box on the wall.

'Nothing. It just won't work.' Alicia watched as he opened it up, studied the timing on it, turned a few buttons and snapped it down again.

Cold air gushed from the vents instantly. 'Your sister is hopeless when it comes to anything mechanical.' He grinned over at Vicky in a conspiratorial kind of way.

Vicky smiled back at him. 'Thanks, Dex. You don't know anything about formulas, do you?'

'Let's have a look.' Dex sat down next to her and pulled the books closer so he could read them.

'That air system is damn well temperamental,' Alicia defended herself swiftly. She felt suddenly helpless. Why did Dex make her feel like that…as if her life wouldn't run smoothly without him? She didn't like the feeling. She had always been independent, needed no one…until she had met him.

'This one isn't right.' Dex pulled a pen through a line of figures. 'Look, there's a very simple way to do this.' He proceeded to do in five minutes what had taken them half an hour.

Alicia wrinkled her nose. 'Coffee, Dex?'

'Thanks, that would be good,' he murmured without looking up.

'Not for me, Alli,' Vicky said swiftly. 'I'm going to have a shower and an early night. I'm shattered.'

Alicia made the coffee, half listening as Dex very gently and patiently explained to Vicky where she had gone wrong with her work. She'd have to tell him about the baby tonight, she told herself forcefully. As soon as Vicky had gone for her shower she would break the news.

She handed Dex his coffee, then sat down next to Vicky, watching as she finished off her work.

Dex glanced across at her. She looked tired, he thought. He'd have to stop putting so much work on her. Sometimes he relied on her too heavily in the office. She was just so efficient, the best secretary he had ever had. He'd have to tread warily; he didn't want to lose her.

He looked from Victoria to Alicia. In some ways they were so alike. Same delicate features, same long, naturally blonde hair. Both wearing shorts and T-shirts. Alicia didn't look much older than Vicky…and Vicky was just a kid really.

'How's that?' Vicky slid the book over towards Dex and he looked at it.

'It's exactly right. You're brilliant,' he enthused.

'No, you're brilliant,' Vicky told him with enthusiastic emphasis. 'I don't know how Alli and I would manage without you.'

He shook his head. 'You'd manage,' he said quietly.

Something about the way he said those words made Alicia's heart squeeze painfully. Maybe they would have to after she'd told him her news. The thing was that Dex didn't love her. This was just an affair. It was wild, exciting, passionate…but it wasn't serious. He had made it clear on several occasions that he didn't intend to settle down and get married. Once he had said that if he did it would be when he was much older, when everything in his life was running smoothly.

'You mean when you've got your pipe and slippers you'll get a wife to match?' she had retorted, her eyes sparkling with amusement.

He had laughed. 'Something like that.'

'Have you ever been serious about any of your girl-friends, Dex?' she had asked suddenly.

His expression had changed. 'I was engaged once…years ago.'

'She must have been very special.'

'She was.' For a moment he'd been quiet, as if far away. 'Clare and I were childhood sweethearts. We were the same age, grew up together, graduated from university together. I knew from a very young age that one day I would ask her to be my wife.'

Alicia remembered feeling hurt for a while. It was all right Dex telling her he didn't want to get serious; she could accept that. She enjoyed their relationship, loved being with him. She was happy with the way things were—after all, she had Vicky to think about. But finding out that Dex had been in love once, had asked that woman to marry him, had made her feel disconsolate, made her wish that she could stir up such powerful emotions within him.

'So what happened? Why didn't you marry her?'

'She died in a car crash on her twenty-third birthday. The morning we were to be married.'

The words had been simply said, with little emotion, yet the expression for one unguarded moment in the darkness of his eyes had been one Alicia would never forget. Her momentary pang of jealousy had melted into compassion. She knew what it was like to lose someone you loved.

'These days I want to put all my commitment into my business,' Dex had continued rapidly, as if speaking about work helped to chase the emotional shadows away from his mind. 'Push my career to the limits, and play the stakes to the highest possible levels. If I had a wife and responsibilities I couldn't take those kind of risks.'

She had gone along with him. 'I can understand that. I don't want to get married either. I'm twenty, Dex…I want a career and travel, success and excitement…'

She had meant those words at the time, but they echoed mockingly in her mind now.

Vicky cleared away all her books as if she was beating the clock, dumped them in her bag and headed for her room. 'I'm just going to make a phone call,' she muttered over her shoulder to Alicia.

Alicia looked across at Dex. He was still wearing the suit he had worn to the office today, she noted. Had he come straight from his meeting with Maddie? If so it had been a hell of a long meeting.

He met her eyes.

'You realise that you're a know-it-all,' she told him lightly.

'I prefer it when you call me a genius,' he said with a grin.

She grinned back at him. 'How did your meeting go, genius?'

'Couldn't have been better.'

'Would you like a glass of wine to celebrate, instead of that coffee?'

'No, thanks. I've already had a glass of champagne, and I've got to drive home.'

She very nearly said, No, you haven't. You can stay here. But she stopped herself. It didn't sound as if he wanted to stay. 'It must have been a terrific outcome if you celebrated with champagne?'

'Nothing is signed yet,' he answered cautiously. 'But I'm quietly confident. I have to go to Perth week after next— meet some of Maddie's associates. I'm hoping to sign a deal while I'm there.'

'Really?' Alicia tried to sound pleased for him.

He nodded. 'I'll be relying on you to hold the fort here for me.'

She didn't say anything.

Dex frowned suddenly. 'Are you OK, Alicia? You look very pale.'

'I'm fine. Just tired.' She got up and went to pour her coffee down the sink. Then stopped with her back to him.

What was she saying? She wasn't fine at all. For a
hormones were up the creek, she had never felt s
emotional. She needed to talk to him. She had to te
before she fell apart.

She turned and looked at him.

'Dex, I have something to tell you.' The words seeme
to come out in a terrible rush.

'It's not about the modelling, is it?' His voice was suddenly wary.

'Modelling?' She stared at him taken aback by the question.

'Peter came in to see me this morning. Early, before you
arrived.'

Alicia frowned. Peter Blake was one of her closest
friends. In a way he was like the big brother she had never
had. He was two years her senior and had grown up in the
same orphanage as she had. He was a talented photographer
now, had made a big name for himself taking terrific shots
of the Queensland scenery.

'He told me about the photographs he had taken of you,'
Dex continued. 'In fact he brought them in to show me.'

'Oh!' She was surprised that Peter had done that behind
her back. She had already told him that she wasn't interested in taking up modelling.

'They were beautiful,' Dex said softly. 'I was impressed.'

'Were you?' She smiled, embarrassed and flattered by
that look in his eye, by that husky quality in his voice.

'He told me that he had sent them to some big agency
in Sydney and they were very interested in you. Then he
accused me of standing in your way, obstructing your road
to a rewarding career.' His voice held an unusually harsh
note. 'I told him that you hadn't even mentioned the offer

start her
over-
him

ink he believed me. Even if he did, he
m me that I was holding you back.'
n.' Alicia pulled away from the sink
by the table. 'He had no right to talk to

going to take up the offer? Go to Sydney?'

She was annoyed with Peter for mentioning this to
She had told him last week, when he had hot-footed
over with the news, that she wasn't interested in leaving
here. Modelling was hardly a secure job; not many girls
made it to the big time. Maybe if she'd been sixteen she
would have stood a better chance, but not at twenty.
Anyway, that was all immaterial now.

'Why not?'

She hesitated. 'For one thing it's not a good time to
uproot Vicky. She's studying for exams.'

'And you want her to have all the opportunities you
never had, don't you, Alli?' he asked gently.

'I want her to do well.' Alicia shrugged.

'There are good schools and great universities in Sydney,
you know.'

She stared at him. 'Do you want me to go?'

There was a moment's silence, and it suddenly occurred
to her that he thought she should take up the offer. Her
heart pounded painfully.

He looked at her, and thought again about how young
she was. 'I want you to do well, be happy,' he said softly.
'You know how ambitious I am, how I'm putting all my
energy into my career. I'd be a hypocrite if I said that's
OK for me but not for you. If you want something you
should go out there and get it. I wouldn't want to stand in
your way…if it's what you want….' He trailed off and
shrugged.

It wasn't what she wanted. She hadn't even given it serious thought. Not because of Vicky, not because she was expecting Dex's baby, but because she couldn't bear to leave him. She loved him with all her heart.

'Strange how paths of opportunity seem to be opening up for both of us at the same time,' Dex continued lightly, when she didn't make any reply.

'Everything happens at once.' She tried to keep her voice light too, but it was laced with emotion even in her own ears. Dex wasn't even a little bit in love with her. He couldn't be, not if he was telling her it was all right if she left. 'Trouble is, those paths seem to be leading off in different directions.'

He reached up and took hold of her hand. The next moment she was sitting on his knee.

'That's better,' he murmured huskily. 'So what are you going to do? Are you going to run off to Sydney and leave me? It sounded like a terrific opportunity the way Peter was talking.'

'I suppose it is.' Her voice was pensive. They should be discussing the baby, but somehow it seemed even harder to bring up the subject now that she knew he wasn't averse to her leaving.

'I suppose if I were to be truthful...not to mention selfish...I'd say I don't want you to go,' he murmured softly.

'You don't?' Her heart missed a beat, her eyes widened as they met his. 'Why?'

'I'd miss you, that's why,' He smiled. 'Apart from anything else, you're the best damn secretary a guy could get.'

Her heart seemed to crash somewhere down near her toes. All right, so maybe a few weeks ago she'd have laughed at that. Now she felt as if she'd never laugh again. 'I'm not going anywhere.'

He frowned as he looked into her eyes and saw the mist of tears there. 'Alicia?'

'I can't go. I'm pregnant.' She whispered the words softly. 'Seven weeks, to be precise.'

She saw shock clearly etched on his handsome face. It was no wonder he was shocked. It wasn't as if they had taken risks. She had been using a contraceptive.

'It's all right,' she said quickly. 'You don't have to offer to marry me or anything...'

He shook his head, seemed lost for words. The expression of shock had been replaced by a look of guilt.

'I'll have to have the baby, of course,' she continued swiftly. 'I mean...I couldn't contemplate the alternative.'

Still he didn't speak.

The silence between them had never been so tense. And yet she continued to sit on his knee.

She reached out and touched his hair. 'I'm sorry,' she said unsteadily.

He closed his eyes. 'Don't say that.'

'Why not? It's how I feel—'

'This is as much my responsibility as yours Alicia,' he said finally, firmly. 'You should have told me earlier.'

'Why?' She looked at him warily.

'Because we've got a lot to sort out.' His voice was calm. 'What do you want to do?'

'I don't know.' She shook her head, then met his eyes directly. 'What do you suggest?'

He frowned, and thought for a moment. The minutes seemed to drag interminably. Alicia suddenly noticed little things, like the tick of the clock on the sideboard, the drip of the tap in the kitchen. Small, inconsequential sounds that normally wouldn't have bothered her. Yet at this moment they seemed so loud they were almost unbearable.

Dex raked a hand through his hair in frustration. He didn't know what to say to her. His eyes moved gently over the pallor of her skin, the wide blue eyes. It was best to be totally honest, he supposed. 'You know I care about you deeply, don't you?' He ran a caressing finger down over the side of her face, but she flinched away from him as if his words had been an insult. He dropped his hand. 'I just don't know if I want marriage—'

'It's all right, Dex.' She cut across him crisply. 'I told you I don't expect you to marry me. I don't think I want to get married.'

He frowned.

'The days of people getting married for the sake of a baby are gone, aren't they?' Alicia stood up. She couldn't think straight when she was so close to him. Her mind was telling her to be practical; her body was telling her something much more emotional. 'We're looking at the twenty-first century, not the Dark Ages.'

'Well…yes.'

Was it relief she could hear in his voice, or perplexity? It was hard to tell what he was feeling. The dark features were so schooled and controlled now.

She went through to the kitchen to tighten the tap and stop the drip. It was more an excuse to turn away from him and collect her thoughts for a moment than anything else.

She had thought about the possible ways this conversation might go many times over this last week. Sometimes she had imagined Dex telling her he had fallen in love with her and asking her to marry him. It was a fantasy. She had always known that the reality was going to be painful.

Dex was also glad of a moment's respite, a chance to gather his thoughts.

Since Peter's visit to his office this morning, his well-ordered, almost phlegmatic life seemed to have been given a good shake. A few realisations had dawned on him, among them the fact that for some time now he had been deliberately avoiding any deep analysis of his feelings for

Alicia. He had been content with the status quo—to remain as it was. He was comfortable around Alicia. He liked and respected her enormously. She was mature for her years, trustworthy, fun, spirited. Perhaps he had been taking her for granted, which wasn't very admirable of him.

It was only when Peter had said she might be leaving that his mind had been jerked awake and he had been forced to look closely at the situation. He didn't want her to leave, was appalled at the prospect. Then guilt had stolen in. Alicia was mature for her years, but that didn't change the fact that she was young, her whole life stretching ahead. He had no right to object to her leaving. Not unless he wanted to make more of a commitment to her. And that was where his dilemma had brooded, and remained too complex to solve.

He cared deeply for Alicia, but as to anything more…he wasn't sure. Love was something he didn't want to speculate on. He didn't know if he was capable of such depth of feeling again. Since Clare he had been so determined not to get too involved, had decided it was better to just play the field and have fun. Dedicate himself to his work. That was when he had decided that if Alicia said she was leaving he'd let her go.

It had been an incredibly hard decision to make, and deep down he had hoped that she wouldn't really want to go.

Now he found out she was pregnant with his child. He didn't know what to do. He wanted to protect her, be with her. But that spelt commitment, and that was the one thing he had told himself he didn't want.

Alicia came back to face him. He noticed how straight she stood, how proudly she held her head.

'Maybe I should just pack things up here, leave Queensland for a while and head for Sydney,' she said suddenly. 'I could model for a few months while I still have my figure, and a new start might be what I need. At least jobs will be plentiful in the city—'

'Don't be crazy.' He cut across her, his voice forceful.

'I'm not crazy.' She glared at him. 'I can manage very well on my own, you know.'

Maybe she could. He knew Alicia didn't lack courage, or determination. His eyes darkened. The thought of her struggling on her own in a big city with his child made a sudden tightness grow in his chest. He pictured the baby going through different stages of development with no influence from a father. Or, worse, Alicia marrying someone else. Someone who would bring his child up. The very thought made him get up from the chair. 'You are not on your own,' he said firmly. 'You've got me.'

Her eyebrows lifted ever so slightly at that.

'We could live together.'

She looked surprised by the suggestion, nearly as surprised as he felt. The idea had flown into his mind from out of nowhere.

She was silent, her heart thumping against her ribs. The idea gave her a moment of pleasure.

'The baby could take my name; we could put it on the birth certificate,' Dex said, warming to the theme. The more he thought of it the more it seemed a practical answer.

She frowned. He would be happy for the baby to have his name, but not for her to have it. That hurt. She shook her head. 'No.' The word came out more vehemently than she'd intended.

'At least think about it.'

'I don't have to think about it. I don't like the idea. For one thing, I don't want my child to have a different name from mine.'

'Why?' He sounded genuinely perplexed. 'It happens a

lot nowadays, and as you said yourself we are in modern times.'

'A few moments ago you were urging me to follow my dream and go to Sydney. Now you're telling me you want the baby to have your name. What next? After it's born are you going to suggest waving goodbye to me and getting a nanny for my baby?'

'That's unfair, Alli. I wouldn't do that. And anyway, I didn't know you were pregnant a few moments ago.'

'Do you like the idea of being a father?' she asked him abruptly.

'Yes,' he answered without reservation, and that took him aback. He frowned. 'Yes…I really do.' He spoke with a kind of wonder that wasn't lost on Alicia.

She was pleased by his reaction, yet saddened by it too. If only he had discovered such a depth of feeling for her.

Dex raked a hand through his hair and continued calmly. 'But I'm not trying to manipulate the situation to get custody of my child—'

'*My* child,' Alicia corrected him quietly. 'I will have sole custody, care and control.'

'Hell, Alli, you're talking as if we're getting a divorce, and we're not even married.'

She shrugged. 'We may as well be honest about things. There's no point in pretending.'

'And living together and giving our child my name will be pretending, will it?' He sounded annoyed now.

'There's nothing wrong with living together. But in our case it will be pretending to have feelings that we just don't have for each other.'

He was grim-faced now.

She waited for a moment, to see if he would argue with her about that, but he didn't. She swallowed on a sudden lump in her throat. She hoped she wasn't going to cry. Her pride was dented enough as it was. 'Well, now that we've examined our feelings for each other, and found them totally lacking in substance, perhaps it would be the right time to end our relationship.' She took refuge behind a bright, flippant tone.

His expression changed to one of incredulity. 'What kind of suggestion is that, when we're going to be parents soon?'

'It's the kind of suggestion a woman makes when she doesn't want to end up feeling used.' Alicia smiled, a crooked, and uncertain smile. 'Better to finish the intimate side of our relationship while we still respect each other and are good friends.'

'We have been good friends, haven't we?' he reflected gently.

'The best.' She took a deep breath. 'Pity we couldn't have fallen in love.'

He stared at her as if she had said something deeply profound.

'Look, I think you had better go,' she said with quiet dignity. She felt that she needed to be on her own now. Console herself, try and and think positively. 'I'm tired, and—'

'Alicia, I don't want our relationship to end.'

'Dex, you're the father of my baby. But as for anything else—'

'Marry me,' he said suddenly.

She stared at him, taken aback, wondering if maybe she had misheard.

He went across and took hold of her by the arms, staring down into her face with earnest eyes. 'I think if I let you walk away from me now, take my child out of my life, it will be something I will always regret.'

'Dex, you don't want to get married...we've been

through this. We've decided that nobody gets married for
the sake of a baby any more—'

'I've changed my mind.' He grinned. 'It's not solely the
prerogative of a woman, you know.'

'Dex, you're acting crazy.'

He shook his head. 'No…I've just realised how much I
want this baby. I've never been more sure of anything in
my life. I want to give him or her a solid home-life, security, love.'

'Very commendable.' Her voice shook with anger. How
dared he talk with such lavish emotion about their baby
and yet propose so coldly to her? 'But *I* can manage to give
my child all the love and security it needs, thank you.' She
didn't want Dex's proposal. She'd rather be on her own
than stuck in a loveless marriage.

'Are you turning me down?' He looked stunned.

If this hadn't been so serious it would have been amusing, she thought. Dex was so supremely confident that it
had probably never occurred to him that any woman could
turn down his proposal of marriage.

'Yes, I'm turning you down.' She stepped away from
him, her head high, her eyes flashing fire. 'I told you I don't
want to get married.'

'You weren't really serious about leaving here… You
can't, not now you're pregnant. You need me.'

'No, I don't,' she snapped positively. She was in love
with him, she wanted him, but she wouldn't lower herself
to accept him on these terms.

'Don't be ridiculous. You can't manage on your own.'

'Dex, we're talking about the rest of our lives. That's
not something that should be decided on a whim. Now I
think you should go.' She needed to get him out of her
apartment fast, while she still had her anger and her pride
to hold on to.

He followed her towards the front door. 'OK,' he agreed with her solemnly. 'It's not something that can be decided rashly.'

'Exactly, and a loveless marriage would just make all of us unhappy.'

She was aware that he was standing very close behind her. As she started to open the door he stretched across her and closed it again.

'But love could grow.' He whispered the words softly, his mouth against her hair, tickling her ear. She could feel the warmth of his body, smell his cologne. 'It isn't something that has to happen instantly, with a crash of cymbals and a choir singing *Hallelujah*.'

Her anger dissolved as quickly as it had erupted. Dex was a realist, a pragmatic businessman. He would think she was the most foolish woman in the world if she were to tell him that her love for him had been instant. From the first moment she had looked into his eyes she had known deep down that this was the man she wanted.

'And to be honest, Alicia, I don't think couples who rush into marriage with love shining a blinding light in their eyes are exactly thinking straight either.' Dex shrugged. 'When the lamplight dims and the magic starts to wane, the survival of any marriage depends on the couple's ability to work at things. Suddenly it boils down to little things, like how much you've really got in common.'

'And how much have we got in common?' Alicia asked him with a wry smile.

'A lot. Don't you see, Alicia? We're good friends; that has to be the most solid foundation of all to build a marriage on.'

'Next you'll be making a computer program of it,' she murmured, a tinge of sarcasm in her voice. 'I can see it now: 'PLAN YOUR COMPATIBILITY BY COMPUTER or HOW TO SURVIVE MARRIAGE USING THE PRAGMATIC PC.'

Dex didn't say anything for a moment. Then he grinned. 'You know, that might be a good idea—'

'Dex, I was joking,' she cut across him impatiently.

'I know you were joking, but it wasn't a bad idea.'

'Except that a computer can't analyse feelings—'

'Or sexual compatibility.' Dex reached to take her hand and turned her to face him. 'I'll have to do some further research into it.' He studied her silently for a few minutes.

Her lips were soft and inviting, her eyes misty with uncertainty. For all her bravado she was scared; he knew that. He bent his head and gently kissed her.

Her lips were sweet and trembling for a moment, then his kiss deepened.

She clung to him, responding hungrily to his touch. Maybe he was right. Marriage was a good solution.

He released her then, and smiled down at her. 'We've certainly got the latter in abundance.'

'The latter?' She couldn't think straight now.

'Sexual compatibility.' He grinned as her cheeks flushed a bright red.

She pulled away from him, her heart pounding. 'But that isn't enough to sustain a marriage, Dex, and you know it.' Her voice was unsteady.

'It's a good start.' He was unrepentant.

'You can't plan a marriage like a business campaign. Any relationship, whether it be living together or marriage, needs love to sustain it.'

He noted the shimmer of tears in her eyes now. 'Oh, sweetheart, don't look at me like that. It breaks my heart,' he said softly. 'I care about you so much…more than any woman in a long, long time.'

'And I care about you.' She lowered her eyes away from him. 'But it's not enough, is it?'

'Look, we're both tired; we need to sleep on things.' His voice was infinitely gentle. 'Let's discuss this over dinner tomorrow night. I'll book a table at Romanio's.'

'I don't know.' His closeness confused her. 'I think we've said all there is to say.'

'Now you know that isn't true.' He traced a finger over the trembling softness of her lips. 'Come on, Alli. I'm just asking you to have dinner with me…please.' His voice was low and huskily inviting. It sent her blood surging through her veins in a way that sizzled.

She nodded. Tomorrow night would be good. Vicky usually went straight to her friend's house on a Friday night. Sometimes she slept over. It would give them time and space to sort something out.

'Thank you.' He bent and kissed her briefly on the lips.

'You won't say anything to anyone, will you, Dex?' she asked him suddenly. 'I mean about the baby. I'd rather wait until further into the pregnancy.'

'That's fine by me.' Dex smiled at her. 'See you in the morning.'

CHAPTER THREE

ALICIA was dealing with an irate phone call from a company who wanted to buy Dex's new computer game. She was being polite and firm, telling them they were launching the product themselves.

At the same time she was filling in a form and running off a letter on the computer.

Dex came out of his office with Maddie McDowell at his side. He smiled at Alicia. 'Fielding nicely,' he murmured as he heard her tell the company that they would keep them in mind for next time.

Alicia put the phone down and grinned. 'Got to keep everyone happy.'

'You could get a gold medal for that,' Dex said, a slightly husky note creeping into the words.

Alicia tried not to blush, aware that Maddie was listening, and said briskly, 'I need you to sign this form when you have a moment.'

'Fine.' Dex reached across and turned the form, signing it with his usual flourish.

'Shouldn't you read that?' Maddie enquired smoothly.

Alicia opened her mouth to tell her that Dex had already vetted it once, but Dex answered before she could get a chance. 'No need. Alicia is a brilliant secretary.' He straightened and smiled. 'Competent, efficient. I trust her implicitly.'

'Really?' Maddie's voice had a slightly wary edge, but her smile didn't falter. 'Good, then we can leave this list in your capable hands.' She put a piece of A4 paper down on Alicia's desk.

'What is it?' Alicia looked down at it, then up at the woman.

Maddie's appearance was as perfect as ever, she noted Her suit was a pale lilac, cool and feminine. Her lipstick, a vivid sweet-pea-pink, seemed to match her perfume, a flowery yet overpowering scent. Her dark hair, as always, sat in a perfect shining bob. Did Maddie never have a bad hair day? Alicia wondered dryly.

'It's a vital list of potential customers that we have to get back to,' Dex answered. 'I need you to put the information on the computer for me.'

Alicia nodded. 'I'll do it straight away.'

'Great. All right, Maddie, we're on track for Tuesday, and our meeting with the accountants, it seems.'

The woman smiled. 'Indeed it does. I'll look forward to it.'

The phone rang and Alicia snapped it up. 'Oh, yes. Hold on a second, I'll see if he's free.' She covered the receiver. 'Your accountant,' she mouthed to Dex.

He nodded. 'I'll take it in my office. See you Tuesday, Maddie.'

As the door closed behind him, Maddie lingered beside Alicia's desk.

Alicia looked up at her.

'Do you think I could have a glass of water?' the woman asked. 'I've got a terrible headache…must be the heat outside.'

'Yes, of course.' Alicia got up and went over to the small room that led off her office, where she made tea and coffee. She took a bottle of mineral water from the fridge and poured a glass. Then brought it back out to Maddie.

The woman smiled at her. She opened a packet of aspirins that she had taken from her handbag and took one with a sip of the water.

'That's much better, thank you.' She put the glass down on the desk, and as she did so her fingers caught on a stack of paperwork sitting there, causing them to fall to the floor in a jumbled heap. 'Oh, no! I'm so sorry.' She bent to try and retrieve them.

'It's OK,' Alicia said soothingly. 'I'll sort it out.'

'Well, if you're sure. I'm really sorry.'

'It will only take me a moment,' Alicia assured her. 'I've got them all numbered.'

'Fine.' The woman stood up, and with a sugary-sweet smile left the office.

It took Alicia longer than she had anticipated to clear the mess. She was still doing it when Dex emerged from his office a while later.

'Hell, what a day,' he muttered. 'I was hoping we would finish a little early.'

'When have you ever finished early?' Alicia smiled.

He thought about that for a moment, then gave a rueful shrug.

'At least you managed to get a lunch-break today.' Alicia finished filing away the last of the papers from the floor and returned to her desk. 'Did you reserve our table at Romanio's?' she asked him casually.

'First thing I did this morning. I'll pick you up at eight.'

She looked up and met his eyes. They had been so busy in the office today there hadn't been a moment to think about their situation, let alone talk about it.

'Fine.' There was a moment's silence. She felt awkward suddenly. It was crazy. They had gone out together for so many meals, yet she felt the strain between them, the knowledge that this date was different.

'I'll just put this information into the computer before I

finish up here.' She changed the subject and reached for the piece of paper that Maddie McDowell had put on her desk. She frowned as she found it wasn't there.

She looked down on the floor under the desk, wondering if it had fallen.

'What's the matter?' Dex asked.

'That list Maddie put on my desk isn't here.'

'It must be there.'

Alicia bit down on her lip, trying to think what could have happened to it. 'Maybe it fell on the floor with the other papers.' She spoke almost to herself.

'Hell, Alicia, that list is important,' Dex grated. 'You could have been more careful.'

'I was careful; it was on my desk, and I haven't touched it.'

'Maybe it floated out of here on its own?' Dex muttered sarcastically.

Alicia glared at him. 'It must have fallen with some papers that Maddie knocked over. Maybe I've filed it mistakenly with one of them.'

Dex shook his head and returned to his office.

An hour later Alicia still hadn't found the list. She had been through every file and frustration was building.

Dex came out as she was starting to go through them again.

'You'd better finish up,' he said gently.

She glanced at her watch. It was almost six-thirty! 'Perhaps you should cancel our table. I don't think I'll be able to relax until I've found this blasted list.'

'Forget the list.' Dex walked across and closed the filing cabinet firmly. 'I don't want to cancel our table.'

She met the dark, intense look of his eyes, and she sighed. 'I don't know where it could have gone, Dex—'

'Look, just forget it now. I'll sort it out. You go home and relax for a while. I'll pick you up at eight o'clock.'

Alicia hesitated, then nodded. She did feel tired. She needed a leisurely shower and a few moments to herself before dinner. It had been a gruelling day.

'OK, see you later.'

As soon as she'd left, Dex started to go through the files himself.

Alicia couldn't stop thinking about that list. It plagued her as she had her shower; it mocked her as she put on her make-up and styled her hair. What on earth could have happened to it? Things didn't just vanish into thin air.

Dex was punctual picking her up. He had changed into a lightweight pair of beige trousers and a khaki-coloured shirt. He looked relaxed, unconcerned as she brought up the subject of the missing list. 'I thought we were forgetting about that,' he said as he opened the passenger door of his car for her.

'I can't.' She waited until he had got into the car beside her before continuing, 'It's just so weird, Dex. I've never lost anything before.'

Dex shrugged. 'You're under a lot of strain…got more important things on your mind, I suppose. Don't worry about it any more. I rang Maddie and she has kept a copy. So it's not a disaster.'

Alicia frowned. 'I may be pregnant, Dex, but that doesn't make me incompetent.'

'I didn't say it did.' He shrugged.

'I just can't think what could have happened to it. One moment it was on my desk…the next gone.'

'Maybe aliens beamed it up.' Dex grinned. 'This could be the first case of industrial sabotage by Martians.'

'A Martian named Maddie, perhaps?' Alicia said lightly.

He looked over at her with a raised eyebrow. 'Now why would Maddie take our list when she was the one who brought it over?'

'I don't know.' Alicia's voice was flat. The idea that Maddie had taken it when she'd been out getting her that glass of water had taken hold as she'd dressed this evening. But she couldn't for the life of her think why the woman would do such a thing.

'Maddie seemed to find the incident amusing,' Dex laughed. 'She reminded me that I had just called you competent and efficient this afternoon…many a word spoken in haste, repented at leisure.'

'I *am* competent and efficient,' Alicia said heatedly.

'Of course you are.' Dex was soothing now. 'Look, let's just forget this. We've got more important things to think about.'

'Yes…you're right,' she agreed.

There was silence as he parked the car.

Romanio's was on the seafront. A delightful restaurant, open to the tropical heat of the night, where candlelight flickered invitingly on the tables.

A waiter showed them to a quiet table in the corner and left them to peruse the menu. Alicia could hear the sound of the sea as it broke against the shore. The night was very still, only the small fan whirring above them on the ceiling broke the heavy feeling in the air.

'Have I told you how beautiful you look tonight?' Dex asked suddenly.

She looked across at him and met his eyes. 'Thank you.' She smiled, feeling shy. She was wearing a pale pink summer dress. It had a round neck and a long skirt. It was feminine and pretty, but she knew she didn't look beautiful.

'How are you feeling?'

She smiled. 'Surprisingly well.'

He shook his head. 'I was thinking about you when I got into bed last night.'

'Oh?' Her eyes lit with amusement. 'Sounds a bit X-certificate. Are you sure you should be telling me this?'

'No, actually, I'm not.' He grinned. 'I kept thinking, I'll have to go easy on Alicia, not put so much work on her shoulders. Then today…what do I do? I pile more than ever on to your desk.'

Alicia laughed at that. 'I'm not ill, Dex.'

'Even so, you must tell me if you can't manage. I can always get a temp in. It's the worst possible time, of course, to make changes in the office, but I don't want you feeling under pressure.'

'Dex.' She leaned further forward. 'Watch my lips. I feel perfectly fine.'

'No morning sickness?'

She shook her head.

'No weird cravings?'

She hesitated, and her lips curved in a teasing smile. 'Nothing I want to admit to in a public place.'

He laughed at that. 'And by the way.' He leaned forward the way she had a moment ago. 'I like watching your lips,' he told her softly. 'They are extremely tempting, kissable lips.'

'It's talk like that that got us into this predicament in the first place,' she joked, yet she felt the heat of longing steal through her at his words, at the look in his eyes.

The waiter came to take their order.

'As I recall you brought me to this restaurant on our first real date,' Alicia remarked when they were left alone again.

'By "real date" I suppose you mean the first time I'd got my nerve up to make a pass at you.' Amusement glinted in the darkness of Dex's eyes for a moment.

'Who are you trying to kid?' Alicia smiled. 'You didn't

need to get up any nerve. You were always a very confident Romeo, Dexter Rowland. I know I had to field a lot of your girlfriends in my first six months of working for you. What was it you used to tell me to say? ''Sorry, he's away at a conference,'' Or the other favourite line, ''He's in a meeting.'''

'Ouch!' Dex grinned. 'But I was nervous about asking you out, Alicia. We'd always been good friends and I was frightened to spoil that.'

'I know what you mean.' Alicia thought back. 'Do you remember when we both worked at MacDales? You always used to say that one day you would leave and start up your own business. We'd loiter over lunch while you dreamed up wild plans for your future, usually culminating in you being worth a fortune before the age of forty.'

'Couldn't I plan anything more original than that?' Dex smiled.

'You were the most ambitious man I'd ever met.'

'You were the most beautiful secretary I'd ever met. I used to envy old Jim MacDale having you floating around his office.'

'No, you didn't. You hardly noticed me back then.'

'So how come I came back to get you once my business was off the ground?' he enquired softly.

'At the time you gave me a lot of convincing spiel about it being good business sense.' She grinned. 'And I knew the work, I was good on computers.'

'Well, there was that,' he acknowledged with a wry smile. 'But it has worked. We've been good together.'

'Yes, I suppose we have,' she acknowledged softly.

'So how about making it permanent?' he asked quietly. 'I meant what I said to you last night. Marry me, Alli.'

Her heart bounced crazily against her chest. 'I know I'm a good secretary, Dex, but you don't need to go to these lengths.' She tried desperately to hide how vulnerable she was behind a screen of light-hearted humour.

'I think I do.' He was very serious.

She was saved from having to make a reply to that by the waiter bringing their meals.

'What do you say?' he prompted her as soon as they were left alone again.

She wrestled with her conscience. She wanted so much to just say yes, but the easy option, the one you wanted with all your heart, wasn't always the right one. 'You've always maintained that marriage wasn't an option for you…or if it was it would be when you're old and grey and settled in your ways.'

'I've changed the plan,' he said wryly.

'For all the wrong reasons.' She toyed with the food in front of her. 'Unlike you, I've had a few weeks to think about this situation, Dex. And, yes, I know we're good together—'

'Wildly good,' he interrupted her, a gleam in his eyes.

She smiled, a tremulous half-smile, as she tried to keep her mind clear. 'Wildly good.' She nodded. 'But it's not enough. I meant it when I said last night that you can't build a marriage without love, and I want everything,' she murmured sardonically. 'Including the band and the crash of cymbals.'

'I'll get down on one knee if you want me to?'

She looked across and met the humour in his expression with a wry smile. 'In my condition that could be dangerous.'

He raised one eyebrow.

'I could fall off the chair in shock.'

'You've got a warped sense of humour, Alli.' He grinned, then reached into his shirt pocket and brought out a small blue velvet box. 'Maybe this will help.'

She looked at him questioningly.

'Aren't you going to open it?'

She reached to pick it up. Inside there was a large solitaire diamond, square-cut, exquisite. It took her breath away.

'The jeweller said that if it doesn't fit you can bring it in and he'll adjust it.'

'It's beautiful, Dex. When did you get it?'

'What do you think I was doing today in my lunch-hour?' he asked with a raised eyebrow. 'You don't think I have time to eat, do you?'

She smiled and closed the box. 'It's a beautiful ring. Thank you, Dex. It's a lovely gesture.' Somehow she kept her voice steady.

He frowned. 'It's not a gesture. It's a proposal—a sincere, serious proposal.'

'But not as sincere as when you proposed once before, to…what was her name? Clare?' For a second she lost control of her voice and it trembled.

His features darkened. 'That was a long time ago. I was another person back then.'

'You were in love; you still remember what it feels like.'

'I remember the pain of losing her.' He spoke bluntly. 'I remember not being in control of my emotions for a long time after her death. If that's what love does to you…' He shook his head. 'I never want to feel that loss again.'

It was the first time he had ever spoken so openly about that period of his life. Alicia felt the rawness in his words, saw it in his eyes. It shocked her. It made her look at him differently. She'd thought she knew him so well…he was the strong businessman, always in control, realistic. But was he that hard-headed? Was this man, who was always so measured when it came to talking about his emotions, simply frightened of letting go…scared of risking love again?

The idea started a flicker of hope within her. If he was serious about marrying her, maybe given time he would fall in love again. Perhaps if she was patient…

She cleared her throat, trying desperately to be sensible, but there was a small voice inside urging her to throw away caution and abandon pride, tell him she had enough love for the two of them.

'I care about you.' Dex's voice was grim. 'I'll look after you, Alicia. That's as much as I can promise…I'm sorry.'

His flat tone dampened her romantic daydreams.

'I don't want to be looked after.' Her voice was quiet, barely audible. She had been 'looked after' in the home where she'd grown up. She knew how miserable life could be without someone who really loved you.

'As I see it, the most important point is that we are expecting a child. We no longer have the luxury of putting ourselves first.'

Alicia didn't say anything. She was tempted to just agree with him. She took a deep breath. 'But the fact remains that if I wasn't pregnant we would never have considered getting married. What we've had has been exciting, but never serious.'

His features tightened. 'If you weren't pregnant you would be skipping off to Sydney, you mean. And our affair, for all its wild excitement, would be forgotten.'

Nothing was further from the truth, but some gleam of pride made her look across the table, meet his eyes and say steadily, 'Maybe you're right.'

She was rewarded by a brief expression of disquiet in the darkness of his eyes. But her small feeling of accomplishment was short-lived. This was too important to play mind games with. 'But let's face it, Dex, the idea of marrying me never crossed your mind before yesterday. So what on earth is the point of rushing into something you don't really want? Especially now.' Alicia picked up her knife and fork and proceeded to eat her meal, although she had absolutely no appetite. She wondered how she was managing to keep so calm…so realistic…when it was nothing to the way her heart felt. 'Your business is in a delicate period of transition. Your finances are stretched.'

'I never realised that finances made such a difference to you.' Dex was very cool now.

'They don't—'

His eyes flicked over the heightened colour in her face. 'Except that Peter has filled your head with ideas of the colossal money to be made as a top model.'

'How many people rise to be top models?' Alicia was dismissive. 'Anyway that has nothing to do with this.'

'Like hell it doesn't.' He stared at her intently. 'You're thinking about not having the baby, aren't you?'

'That couldn't be further from the truth.' She was horrified by the suggestion.

'So why won't you marry me?'

She put down her cutlery and leaned back in her chair. 'I've told you. Because it doesn't feel right.'

'I'm not always going to be strapped for cash, Alicia,' he said seriously. 'I'm going to be very successful. You do believe in me, don't you?'

'Of course.' She looked across at him earnestly. 'This has nothing to do with money or success or power, or anything like that, it's to do with you and I.'

He didn't look convinced. There was silence for a while. She put her knife and fork straight on her plate; she couldn't eat anything more, felt that if she had another mouthful of food it might stick in her throat.

'Do you want to order something else?' he asked.

She shook her head.

'You should eat something more, you need to keep your strength up.'

Alicia's lips twisted in a wry smile. 'I can take care of myself, Dex. You don't have to start worrying about me.'

He put up his hand and summoned the waiter. 'Do you think we could have the bill, please?' he asked politely.

Looking across at him now, Alicia could see a shuttered expression on the handsome face. He seemed withdrawn, remote.

'Dex, don't be angry with me,' she said quietly. 'How can I agree to something when I know deep down it just isn't going to work?'

He didn't say anything to that.

She watched as he paid the bill and then picked up the ring box from the table. 'Let's go, shall we?'

Numbly she followed him out of the restaurant. They crossed the quiet road towards the car.

It was a clear, moonlit night. The sea looked a silver colour, and the palm trees that lined the beach were dark silhouettes.

There was a children's playground under the trees. A couple were pushing a little girl on a swing and her laughter drifted on the night air. It was the only sound except for the sea.

They got into the car, but Dex didn't start the engine right away.

'We could be like them.' Dex nodded his head in the direction of the couple.

She felt her heart squeeze inside.

'But you're throwing it all away.'

She couldn't answer him, couldn't find the strength to answer him.

'OK we don't love each other,' he grated. 'But we're friends…we're good together in bed.'

'Too good.' It took a lot to find the fortitude to joke now.

'I want our baby, Alicia.'

'I know.' Her voice was very quiet. He wanted the baby more than he wanted her.

'But what happens after you get bored with the good sex?' Her voice crumbled. 'I mean, I suppose, apart from Clare, you've never kept a girlfriend past a few months, Dex.'

'You mean when you're past your sell-by date?' He grinned, with a return to his good humour.

'Something like that.' Her lips twisted in bitter amusement.

'OK, since Clare I've never wanted to settle down… But then I never figured I'd be this excited about becoming a dad.'

Something about the way he said those words made her want to melt inside.

She made no effort to resist as he took her into his arms.

He found her lips and kissed her, a long, sweet kiss that made her senses reel.

She felt his hands on her body, stroking her, caressing her.

Her breathing was uneven; she could feel her heart pumping against the silky coolness of his hand.

Her heart was his; it always had been. He only had to lay a hand on her to stake his claim.

'Marry me, Alli, and I'll make you happy. We'll have good sex, lots of money and even more babies, if you want!'

She laughed through a shimmer of tears. 'What a proposal! You're crazy, Dexter.'

'Can I take that as a yes?' He pulled away to look at her. The car was in darkness, and all he could really see was the vivid glitter of her blue eyes.

'I think you can,' she admitted softly.

Who was she kidding? she wondered with bittersweet satire. The answer had always been yes. She had just been hoping... Her breathing faltered; her mind clouded. She had just been hoping for the impossible...that Dex would say he loved her. But she supposed numbly that you couldn't have everything...

CHAPTER FOUR

'IS HE in?' Maddie McDowell swept into the office. She looked radiantly lovely in a chic yellow suit.

'Yes—'

'Good.' The woman turned for Dex's office door without waiting for Alicia to ring through and tell him he had a visitor.

'Oh, by the way.' She turned, her dark hair swinging in a fluid silky movement, her hand on the door handle. 'I believe congratulations are in order.' Her eyes moved to the engagement ring on Alicia's finger.

'Yes, thank you.'

'Of course it won't be easy.'

Alicia frowned. 'What do you mean?'

'I mean marriage isn't easy.' The woman put her hand on her hip. 'What did you think I meant?'

Alicia shrugged, uncomfortably aware that for a second she had feared this woman might know that she was pregnant. That would have hurt. Dex had promised he wouldn't tell anyone until after their wedding…not even Vicky.

Maddie's eyes narrowed for a second, then scarlet lips curved in a pleased smile. 'Don't mind me. I'm just an old cynic. I've been married once, and the experience was not pleasant.'

Old indeed! The woman could only be in her early thirties.

'Of course, you are getting Dex, and he's simply gorgeous. You realise you're the envy of every woman in Queensland?'

'Am I?' Alicia forced herself to smile.

'Oh, yes. Dex is quite a catch. Apart from the fact that he's exceptionally good-looking, his prospects are very rosy. I reckon he'll be a millionaire before he turns forty.'

'Maybe...maybe not.' Alicia shrugged. 'Money isn't everything. I'm marrying Dex because I love him.' How come she was able to tell the truth so easily to this stranger and yet she couldn't say the words to Dex? she wondered angrily. Pride could be a very bizarre emotion, she decided.

Maddie laughed. 'In a world where money and power are the main aphrodisiacs, how delightfully old-fashioned of you.'

'That may be the world as you see it, but it's certainly not my perception,' Alicia said quickly. 'And I don't think it's Dex's either.'

Maddie's eyebrows rose. 'Most men are turned on by success and power. I'm sure Dex is no exception. Well, actually I know he's not.'

Alicia frowned.

'He's very ambitious,' Maddie continued airily. Then she shook her head. 'But I shouldn't be rubbing my cynicism in the face of your happiness. It's tacky of me, forgive me. I'm sure you'll be very happy with Dex. He'll make a dutiful husband and a good father, I'm sure.'

Alicia felt her cheeks growing very hot at those words.

Maddie's smile widened. 'Oh, by the way.' She opened up her handbag. 'Before I forget. Here's a copy of the list that you lost the other week. Very careless of you, Alicia, especially after Dex gave you such glowing references.'

She spoke as if she had been given the sack. Glowing references indeed! 'I'd say it was more strange than careless.' Alicia answered briskly. 'The list never did show up. It's almost as if someone took it.'

'Really?' The woman shrugged. 'You'd better be on your guard, then. It could be industrial sabotage.'

Dex's office door opened and closed behind her.

'Or it could have been you, trying to undermine me,' Alicia muttered to herself. Or was she just becoming paranoid? She let her breath out in a long sigh. A moment ago she had wondered if Maddie knew she was pregnant. That remark about Dex being a good father had been odd. But she couldn't possibly know…unless Dex had told her? Fury ate through her at the notion.

She stared at the computer screen in front of her and tried desperately to concentrate purely on work.

An hour later the office door opened and Maddie and Dex came out.

'OK, so we're agreed on those figures?' Dex was saying crisply.

'Yes, all agreed.' Maddie smiled up at him. 'We'll talk about it tomorrow over lunch.'

'Fine.'

Smiling, Maddie put down a stack of papers on Alicia's desk. 'Be a dear and make some copies of these, will you, Alicia?' she said, heading towards the door, then turned suddenly. 'You won't lose them, will you?'

Alicia felt herself clenching her teeth. 'I'll try not to.'

'Great. I'll pick them up tomorrow.'

'Just who does she think she is?' Alicia demanded of Dex as soon as the door had closed behind her.

'It's just a few copies. Do it for her tomorrow if you have time.'

'She acts as if she's my boss,' Alicia said, shaking her head. 'And she's not! I won't have it.'

'OK, point taken.' Dex looked uncomfortable for a moment. Then he leaned forward and looked at her screen. 'Are you putting that list she gave you on to the computer?'

'I've already done it,' Alicia told him brusquely. 'And I think the way that piece of paper disappeared is most odd.'

'Yes…we won't go into that again.' Dex said with equal firmness. He tapped the papers Maddie had put down on her desk. 'Do you think you could put these on disk for me before you copy them for Maddie?'

'I'll do it now.'

'Great.' With a pleased smile Dex went back into his office. Alicia got back to her work, closing out Maddie from her thoughts with grim determination.

She had finished everything by the time Dex came back out again.

'Have I ever told you that you're indispensable?' Dex said with a grin as he watched her bustling around the office, filing the disks away.

I suppose that's the nearest I'll get to a declaration of love, Alicia thought wryly. She turned and smiled at him. 'Can I have that in writing?'

'No, you'll only want a raise.' He laughed.

'You've found me out.'

His eyes moved over her figure in a brief appraisal as she bent to lock the filing cabinet. She was wearing a heather-pink dress, plain yet stylish. Her long blonde hair was tied back from her face in a thick French plait that fell down her back.

'Of course, I'm always willing to negotiate,' he said smoothly.

'Open to persuasive measures, eh?' Alicia said playfully. 'I'll have to bear that in mind. How about coming around to my place tonight? I'll cook dinner.'

He paused. 'I'd love to…but actually I've got a business dinner to go to.'

'Oh…maybe you can come over later?'

He frowned. 'I'm really tired, Alli, and I've another meeting first thing in the morning.'

She nodded and pretended not to care, but she did. They hadn't slept together since she had told him she was pregnant, and that was over two weeks ago. She was missing him.

She crossed back towards her desk. 'Dex, did you tell Maddie that I'm pregnant?' she asked, trying to sound nonchalant.

'No! Why?'

Alicia shrugged. 'Just a feeling I got…she seemed to know.'

'I haven't said anything.'

Alicia frowned and looked down at her slim figure. 'It's not as if I'm showing or anything, is it?' She looked sharply up at Dex. 'I don't look fat, do I?'

He laughed at that, and reached to get hold of her hand as she passed by him. 'No, you don't.' He pulled her close and kissed her full on the lips. Immediately she felt her annoyance and her worries melt away.

'You're beautiful,' he murmured.

'Am I?' She cuddled closer and kissed him back.

'Yes, and I can't wait to make you my wife.'

'Oh, Dex!' Now she was crying.

'What is it?' He looked down at her in alarm, searching for a handkerchief and mopping up her tears with gentle, sweet concern. 'Why are you crying?'

'I don't know.' She looked up at him and laughed through the haze of tears. 'Must be my hormones. Pity you can't have them extracted like teeth,' she complained. 'I've never felt so…so vulnerable in all my life.'

'It will be OK.' He held her close.

Even through her brief feeling of happiness she felt a

tinge of uncertainty about that. How would it be all right
when he just didn't love her?

'Tell you what. Let's pack in here early. I've got something I want to show you.'

'What?'

'It's a surprise.' He pulled back from her. 'Switch off
your computer, switch on the answering machine and we'll
go.'

Twenty minutes later they were driving down the Cook
Highway. The sky was an intense, almost electric blue, and
the green fields of sugar-cane that lined the road swayed in
the soft balmy breeze blowing in from the ocean.

Dex turned off the main road and took a winding lane
down towards the sea. He pulled to a halt by a small deserted cove.

'What are we doing here?' Alicia asked as they left the
air-conditioned cool of the car.

'What do you think?' Dex asked her gently.

'I think it's beautiful.' Alicia looked down at the white-
capped waves thundering in against the creamy line of the
shore. She could taste the salt on her lips, smell the tangy
scent of the gum trees that lined the beach.

'You're not looking in the right direction,' Dex said as
he came around to her. He put his hands firmly on her
shoulders and turned her away from the sea.

Behind them a small driveway wound its way up towards
a cottage. It was quite simply adorable. Built on stilts, it
had a wrap-around porch, white walls and vivid green shut-
ters. A bright red 'For Sale' sign had a sticker across it
marked 'SOLD'.

'What do you think?' Dex asked her again. He was
watching her intently.

'I don't understand.' She frowned and turned to look
at him.

'It's ours. I signed the contract yesterday.'

Her eyes widened.

'I had to move fast because there was someone else interested in it. You do like it?' For the first time uncertainty clouded his bright confidence.

'Yes, of course I like it.' She took a deep breath. 'But I'd have liked it even more if we'd chosen it together.'

'I wanted it to be a surprise.' He frowned. 'I thought you'd be happy.'

'I am.'

'You don't sound it.' His voice was grim, hard with disappointment.

Alicia tried to rally her thoughts. She was upset that he had made such a major decision without consulting her...but in all honesty that was so like Dex. He was so positive, so sure of himself. 'It's a wonderful surprise,' she said brightly. 'I...I'm just a bit stunned, that's all.'

'I remembered you telling me once that your dream house would have a wrap-around porch and a view to die for,' he said, regaining his good humour. 'And it certainly has a good view. The back looks right up towards the rainforest.'

Her eyes moved over his face as he spoke. He was so dear to her. Really they could have lived in a tent and she would have been happy.

He looked back down at her and smiled. 'And it's got three bedrooms. One for us, one for Vicky and one for junior.'

She smiled back. 'Thank you, Dex. It will be our first real home for a long, long time.' She stood on tiptoe and kissed him on the lips. The kiss deepened. She could taste the salt on his lips. The sound of the waves crashing against the shore filled her mind, her senses.

'Come and have a look inside.' Dex pulled back from her and caught hold of her hand.

Together they walked up the driveway and up the steps to the front door.

Alicia waited as he found the correct key for the lock and the door swung open. She was about to go in ahead of him when he stopped her. 'Let's do this right, shall we?' He grinned, and then swept her up into his arms to carry her over the threshold.

'Aren't you supposed to carry me over the threshold when we're newly married?' she asked with a laugh as she wrapped her arms around his neck.

'Not sure. But we've done everything else back to front. Why not this?'

'Why not?' she agreed.

He put her down and she looked around. The house was empty, and the rooms seemed very big after her small apartment.

The floors were a polished cedar, the windows looked down towards the cove and out over the blue of the sea towards the Great Barrier Reef.

'It's fabulous,' she sighed. 'Can we afford it?'

'I hope so.' He laughed. 'We might have to tighten our belts for a while, but I reckon it will be a good investment.'

Her eyebrows lifted at that. 'I think I might have to let my belt *out* for a while,' she said, patting her stomach.

He laughed. 'We'll manage.' He reached across and took hold of her hand. 'You'll be happy to know that the bank manager has a lot of faith in my business acumen.'

'I'm no longer alone in thinking you're a genius, then?' she asked playfully.

'Oh, no.' He shook his head. 'There are a growing number of converts every week, it seems.'

He pulled her hand. 'Come and have a look at the master bedroom; it has an *en suite* bathroom.'

'Pity there's no bed,' Alicia murmured as they walked into the large room. 'We could have christened the place properly.'

'We'll go shopping next week,' he promised.

It crossed Alicia's mind that at one time it wouldn't have mattered if there wasn't a bed. He'd have taken her right here, right now.

'We should measure the windows for curtains,' she said, turning her mind away from that thought. They had other, more practical things to think about, she told herself swiftly. Their wedding was just under two weeks away, and if they wanted to move straight in here they would have to get organised.

'I've already taken the measurements. They're in the glove compartment of the car,' he answered her, with his head inside one of the fitted wardrobes as he tried to see what was wrong with the hinges on the door.

'You're so organised. Next you'll be telling me you've chosen the soft furnishings,' she murmured wryly.

He closed the wardrobe doors and turned to look at her with a grin. 'No, I'll leave all that up to you. You'll have plenty of time. I'm flying out to Perth day after tomorrow. I'll be gone for a week.'

'A week!'

'I've a lot of business to sort out, Alli. Don't look so shocked. I did tell you a while ago that I had to go.'

'Yes.' Alicia's hands curled tightly in, so that her nails dug against the soft skin of her palms. 'Is Maddie going with you?'

'Of course.' He frowned. 'I told you, she's setting up some meetings for me with her associates. This is a very important trip.'

'Yes, I realise that.' Alicia forced a stiff smile to her lips. She knew this was business, and she trusted Dex, she told herself firmly. She just wished she didn't feel so damn jealous.

It wasn't often that she took a dislike to someone, but she had with Maddie McDowell. It was unfortunate that Maddie seemed to be the one person that Dex needed.

The notion was a discomfiting one.

'Dex?'

'Yes?' He was examining one of the catches on the windowframe now.

She watched him silently for a moment. He had his back to her. He looked so handsome, she thought suddenly. The light business suit looked good on him, defined the breadth of his shoulders, the powerful physique.

'What is it?' He turned and gave her his full attention.

'Make love to me.' Her voice echoed in the empty house.

'What, now?'

She smiled. 'Why not?' She walked over to him and curved her hands up around his shoulders, looking up at him with eyes that were a vivid hyacinth-blue.

'Alli, I—'

As he started to say something she took his hand and placed it over her breast. He could feel the heat of her body through the thin material.

She left his hand and reached to unfasten his tie. Then she started to unbutton his shirt.

'Hell, Alicia.' He muttered, lowering his head. 'You're a wild cat sometimes.'

'Is that good or bad?' She kissed his neck, stroked her hand down through the dark hair on his chest.

'Sometimes good...sometimes bad.' He grinned as she pulled back from him and looked reproachfully up into his eyes.

'Only bad when I've got to be somewhere else.' He kissed her softly on the lips. 'And I've got an appointment in under an hour.'

'Plenty of time,' she murmured huskily, kissing him back.

'Maybe you're right.' His hands curved around her waist, lifting her to lean her against the wall. Then he kissed her again, and the heat of his kiss made her body temperature rise sharply.

His hands moved over her body, exploring, persuasive. For a while they were lost to each other; only their breathing and the sound of the sea outside encroached.

'I shouldn't really be doing this,' he murmured huskily against her ear. 'I've got responsibilities now.' His hand stroked down over her stomach. 'I should be running to that meeting, working extra hard because only the best will be good enough for junior.'

'Very admirable.' She kissed his ear. 'I'm just a bad influence.'

'Wicked,' he growled. 'But I'm going to have to summon up every ounce of will-power from somewhere.' He found her lips, and the kiss was sweet, but at the same time he was fastening the buttons on her dress.

'Do you have to?' she murmured shakily as he pulled away from her.

'Afraid so. This meeting is important. Maddie will expect me to attend; she's set it up.'

'Dex!' She was annoyed for a moment as she watched him buttoning up his shirt.

Maybe Maddie had been right when she had said today that money and power were what really turned him on.

Maddie had both of those attributes in abundance.

He kissed her softly. 'I'll make it up to you, Alli. Promise.'

CHAPTER FIVE

THE front doorbell rang as Dex was adjusting the flower in his buttonhole.

He glanced at his watch, hoping he wasn't running late. Surely wasn't his best man. He wasn't due for another half-hour. Quickly he left his bedroom and strode across to open the door.

'Maddie!' He stepped back in surprise.

She laughed. It was a tinkling, attractive laugh. 'I know it's bad luck to see your bride on the morning of the wedding, but the same doesn't apply to your business associate…at least I don't think it does. You're safe to invite me in.'

'Of course, come in.'

She was wearing a pale blue suit and a big picture hat which framed her pretty face perfectly.

'You look lovely,' he remarked.

'Thanks. Thought I'd make a special effort as it's your big day.'

He noted the husky quality in her voice and frowned. 'Would you like a drink?' he asked politely.

She nodded. 'Something strong.'

He watched as she sat down on the settee, crossing long legs. She was wearing impossibly high stiletto heels. 'I'm expecting Steve…my best man…any minute,' he said as he crossed to the drinks cabinet.

'Oh…OK. I won't stay long.' Her eyes darted to where his overnight case stood packed and ready by the door. 'We don't want people to talk…do we? Especially on the morning of your wedding.' She slanted a mischievous look up at him as he handed her the drink. 'Not joining me?'

'I think I'll keep a clear head,' he said with a smile.

Her eyes flicked over him. He looked extremely handsome in the dark suit. Tall, powerful and incredibly sexy.

'I just want to talk to you about what happened in Perth,' she said quietly.

Dex hesitated before replying. 'I don't think now is the right time for business. We'll discuss it in the office when I get back.'

'I wasn't going to talk about business and you know it.' Her eyes flashed fire.

'Look Maddie—'

'And there isn't going to be a "right time" after this afternoon, is there?' She silenced him with her tearful tone, then bit down on her lower lip. 'I mean you're getting married, for heaven's sake!'

He frowned.

'Have you told Alicia that we once had an affair?'

'Why should I? Our affair was over a long time ago. I don't see that there's anything to be gained by raking over it. In fact it will just make our working relationship untenable.'

She took a sip of her drink, then put it down and got to her feet. 'I understand why you're being like this.' She placed one hand on the material of his jacket, stroking the silky weave with long, scarlet-tipped fingers. 'Really I do. Alicia's pregnant, isn't she?'

He frowned. 'How do you know that?'

'Call it a woman's intuition.' Maddie smiled. 'I saw her coming out from her doctor's a few weeks ago. Then you were planning this whirlwind wedding.'

'I'd appreciate it if you would keep your ideas on the

subject to yourself, Maddie. I don't want to talk about Alicia.' His voice was quiet and firm.

'Neither do I.' Maddie breathed the words huskily, then stood on tiptoe to kiss him.

'Maddie.' He put his hands on her arms and moved her back. 'What happened between us is in the past. I thought we were both in agreement about that before we started to do business together.'

'Yes, but then we kissed in Perth, and I thought you were regretting that decision as much as I was.' Maddie looked up at him from beneath long dark lashes.

'Look, it was a moment when neither of us was thinking straight. You were thrilled with the way our business meeting had gone. You threw your arms around me and the next moment you kissed me—'

'You kissed me back.'

'Yes, I did.' His voice was quiet, gentle. 'And I'm really sorry if I misled you. It was an impulsive, instinctive reaction. It was one kiss and it meant nothing.'

'Liar.' Maddie smiled provocatively.

'Stop it, Maddie.' Dex's voice was firm, and more than a little angry now. 'I'm getting married in just over an hour's time, and I don't need or want this kind of complication in my life.'

'I notice you aren't telling me how much you love your bride-to-be,' Maddie said bluntly. 'I don't think your feelings are very strong for her at all.'

Dex stared at her. 'That's just where you're wrong. I told you in Perth. My days of casual affairs are over.'

There was a flicker of uncertainty on the attractive face, then she laughed. 'Bravo. I almost believed you for a minute.'

The doorbell rang. Dex moved away from her.

As he reached to open the door a memory hit him from

out of nowhere. It was as if he was transported back in time
for just an instant, to the morning of the day he should
have married Clare. He remembered how joyfully he had
swung the door open, only to be faced with the news of
Clare's death. His hand tightened on the door handle; he
felt the blood draining from his face. If anything had happened to Alicia... His heart stilled...

Peter Blake stood outside. He grinned and tapped the
large professional camera he was carrying. 'Just called to
take a couple of photographs of you and the best man...'
His voice trailed off and he frowned. 'You OK, mate? You
look as if you've seen a ghost.'

Alicia studied her reflection in the mirror. She hadn't chosen a traditional wedding dress; instead she wore a long
butter-gold dress in Thai silk. Embossed into the silky
weave of the material were thousands of small, shimmering
white daisies. It was unusual; it was stunning. The square
neckline of the bodice ran to a sharp V at her waist, en-
hancing the soft swell of her breasts, her narrow waist,
before falling in a full skirt to the floor.

She didn't look pregnant, she reassured herself. No one
would guess that she was now nearly eleven weeks.

'You look so beautiful,' Vicky said in a whisper from
behind her.

Alicia turned and smiled at her sister. 'Thank you. So do
you,' she said honestly.

Vicky did look lovely in her white bridesmaid's dress,
with a simple gold band of silk around her waist in the
same material as Alicia's dress.

'I'm so happy that you're marrying Dex.' Vicky smiled.
'I think you're perfect for each other.'

'I hope so.' Alicia felt a tremor of nerves run through

her. She couldn't believe that it was her wedding day.
Everything had been arranged so quickly.

It was under a month since Dex had asked her to marry
him. They had a house, they had the rings…all that remained was to pledge their vows this afternoon at the small
chapel by the sea.

'I'm scared to death,' she admitted now to Vicky in the
privacy of the small bedroom in their apartment.

Vicky looked at her. 'You know, this is the first time
I've ever heard you admit to being afraid,' she said gently.
'Even when Mum and Dad died you were the strong one,
the positive one…because you had to be, for me.'

Alicia smiled. 'I'm the big sister. I'm just better at boss-
ing you around.'

'That's true.' Vicky laughed. 'But I'm grateful to you,
sis, for all you've done for me. For being the heroic big
sister who took care of me. I'm just so pleased that now
you're going to have someone in your life who can be
strong for *you*,' Vicky continued. 'Dex really loves
you…don't be scared, put your trust in him. You deserve
to be happy.'

Alicia reached to embrace her sister, and for a while the
two of them stood locked in each other's arms.

Vicky thought she was just suffering from normal pre-
wedding nerves. If only things were that simple, Alicia
thought sadly. She was glad that her sister had no idea of
the truth. Her romantic illusions would be shattered if she
knew Dex had never spoken a word of love to her…that
his reasons for proposing were all logical and practical.
That his one true love had been Clare, and no other woman
would ever take her place in his heart.

She shouldn't be thinking about that, not this morning.
'You're right, I shouldn't be scared,' she said brightly as

they pulled apart. She reached for some tissues to dry her eyes. 'How did someone of sixteen get so wise?'

Vicky grinned. 'I'm seventeen next week, sis. I hate to remind you but I'm all grown up.'

The shrill ring of the doorbell interrupted them. Vicky glanced at her watch. 'That will be Peter. I'll let him in.'

Alicia nodded. Peter had agreed to give her away. He was also taking the photographs for them as a wedding present.

She heard Peter's cheerful voice and checked her make-up before going out to face him. Good thing she had used waterproof mascara, she thought wryly.

She stared at her face, but she was thinking about Vicky's words. ''Dex really loves you...put your trust in him.''

Her heart pounded painfully. Maybe one day Dex would fall in love with her. That hope was the only thing getting her through, was the main reason she had agreed to marry him.

She kept telling herself that he just needed time.

She hoped she wasn't fooling herself. But, as Vicky had said, she just had to place her trust in him now.

Maybe the situation might have been helped if she could have thrown away her own foolish pride and told him how much she loved him, instead of pretending that it was the baby that was keeping her here.

Trouble was, she had real difficulty speaking words of love. She found it hard to let go and put her trust completely in someone. She had been hurt so many times in her young life. First when her parents had died, and secondly by the string of people who'd been supposed to care for her in her youth. It seemed that every time she got close to someone they went away. It had toughened her...made her over-wary.

Was that what was causing these fears now about Maddie McDowell? She had imagined so many horrible things in the week Dex had been away with her in Perth. Had imagined them together in ways that had made her body burn with anguish. And Dex had been so distant since he had returned. Of course there hadn't been time for them to talk…not really talk…and that hadn't helped. There had just been so much to do, organising the wedding.

'Alicia,' her sister called her. 'Time is moving on.'

'Coming.' Alicia reached for her bouquet. She would make Dex a good wife, she told herself positively. She was going to make this marriage work.

The small chapel was in an idyllic setting, surrounded by palm trees between the sugar fields and the shore. The afternoon was languid, the sun dazzling.

Peter took so many photographs that she felt almost dizzy.

'Shouldn't we go in now?' she said, looking towards the waiting open wooden door. The thought that everyone was inside waiting for her was daunting.

'In a minute.' Peter grinned. 'The bride should always be ten minutes late…it makes the groom all the keener.'

Alicia wasn't so sure about that. She wondered what Dex was thinking…was he nervous? Was he regretting his decision to marry out of obligation, duty? This was the time when practical thoughts could be deserting him, replaced by memories of how love should feel.

'Just a couple more shots,' Peter assured her, angling his professional camera and snapping furiously. 'You look so gorgeous…' he drawled. 'Come on, toss that blonde hair of yours and give me another of those smouldering looks.'

'This is for a wedding album,' Alicia reminded him, trying to laugh, trying to push her anxieties away. 'Not a glossy magazine.'

'Sorry, can't help myself.' He grinned as he handed his camera to his assistant.

Peter hadn't stopped rhapsodising over her dress and her looks since setting eyes on her at the apartment. Nor had he stopped talking about the opportunity waiting for her in Sydney.

Alicia looked up at him with affection. He was very handsome in his dark suit. She was unused to seeing him so smart. Usually Peter slopped around in shorts and T-shirts. He'd even had his blond hair cut, much to her astonishment.

She was flattered that he had gone to so much trouble for her.

'I just want the best for you, Alicia,' he told her gently now. 'You and Vicky are the closest thing to family that I've got. And if you ever need anything, I'll be there for you.'

'I know, and I appreciate it, Peter.'

He smiled. 'Now we've got the slushy stuff over, shall we get on with the important business of the day?' He nodded towards the church door. 'Ready?'

She faltered, her heart thundering suddenly in her breast. 'Ready as I'll ever be.'

There weren't many people in the church. Just their closest friends and Dex's parents, who had flown in from America that morning.

The beautiful strains of Mendelssohn's 'Wedding March' filled the church as she stepped in, and the congregation rose to their feet.

The church smelt of candle-wax and the heavy scent of lilies. Alicia looked up and saw Dex waiting for her.

She forgot everyone else when he turned and smiled. This was right…this was the man she loved with all her heart.

As she reached his side he took hold of her hand. The touch of his skin against hers made her body burn.

He squeezed her hand gently, and the feeling that flowed through her was electric.

Throughout the wedding service Alicia couldn't take her eyes from Dex. They exchanged their vows as if they were the only two people in the world, and Alicia's voice was clear and certain in her promises.

'With my body I thee worship…'

She saw the gleam of dark approval in Dex's eyes, and for just a moment her voice faltered. When she stepped out of this dress tonight she would be his, body and soul. It would be the first time they had made love since she had told him about the baby. She wanted to give herself to him so much. Her body yearned for his touch, for his possession, for his love.

'With my body I thee worship…' Dex's voice was firm and serious.

Were all the vows he made being taken solely out of duty? She searched his face, looking for some sign, some hint that this marriage wasn't just about giving his baby a settled home and a name. It was hard to see what exactly he was thinking; he looked so stern, so resolute.

Then he slipped the gold wedding band on her finger. It felt cold against the warmth of her skin.

'I pronounce that you be man and wife together.'

Alicia smiled tremulously up at her new husband. He didn't smile back; his eyes were dark with some emotion she couldn't read.

Then he bent and kissed her. His lips were dominant and possessive. They captured hers in a sensual caress that made her breathing quicken, made her feel light-headed with the force of her need for him.

He smiled as he pulled back from her. There was an

expression almost of triumph on the lean, handsome face, as if he was fiercely glad that the vows had been taken, that she was legally his.

Her heart leapt wildly in response.

When they stepped outside the church, confetti was thrown in a wild mosaic of colour. It splashed over the couple, landing in Alicia's hair and dress, sprinkling colour over Dex's dark jacket.

Dex kissed her again, and then his lips moved to whisper against her ear. 'Thank you.'

'For what?' She looked up at him, perplexed.

'For saying yes. For making me a very happy man.'

'Oh, Dex.' Her eyes sparkled with tears. She stood on her tiptoes and kissed him gently on the lips.

'I can't wait to get you away from all of these people,' Dex murmured in a low tone, as Peter's camera clicked, capturing every moment. 'Get you out of that dress, gorgeous as it is.'

Her cheeks coloured slightly. The thought of being alone with him, of celebrating their vows, filled her with nervous but sweet anticipation.

Dex's parents came over to congratulate them. Alicia smiled shyly at them. Dex was like his father, she noted. He had the same strong build, the same distinguished good looks. His mother was younger than she had imagined, she could only have been in her late forties.

To Alicia's delight they both embraced her warmly, their wishes for future happiness sincere and effusive. Alicia immediately liked them.

They were interrupted by Peter, who wanted them to pose for more photographs.

Then it was on to the hotel for a buffet reception.

The Bay Hotel had spectacular views out over the ocean, and there was a relaxed, happy atmosphere as the wedding guests circulated freely. Alicia enjoyed getting to know Dex's parents; hearing little snippets of information about Dex's youth was very entertaining.

'So he hasn't always been the cool, level-headed businessman,' Alicia said, laughing as his mother told a tale from his wild student days.

'Dex has always been good fun.' Barbara Rowland smiled. 'I'm just so glad that he has fallen in love again and has decided to settle down. I was so worried about him after he lost Clare.'

'It was very sad,' Alicia said softly.

'I shouldn't be talking about Clare, should I?' his mother said quickly, anxiously. 'Not today…not when you're both so happy. It's insensitive of me. Forgive me.'

'It's all right, really, Barbara.' Alicia's tone was reassuring. 'In fact I'm glad you mentioned her. Dex finds it difficult to talk about the past, and I don't press the subject because I think it's painful for him. But I've often wondered about her. What was she like?'

Dex's mother hesitated for a moment. 'She was like a member of the family. Her parents were our very good friends and we watched her grow up. Neither Dex nor Clare had eyes for anyone else. When she died it was as if a light had been turned out inside Dex. He was devastated. Even when he eventually started to date again all the girls he was drawn to looked a bit like Clare—dark hair, green eyes. It was as if subconsciously he was searching for her. I think the reason he left Boston and the States was a desire to get away from everything and just start again.' Barbara smiled. 'And he has succeeded—put the past behind him and fallen for the most beautiful girl. I couldn't be more happy.'

'Yes…' Alicia's smile was somewhat tremulous for a second. She glanced around, wondering where Dex had got to. She wanted him beside her suddenly. Wanted to feel his arm around her. She caught sight of him talking to Maddie at the other side of the room.

It had been Alicia's idea to invite Maddie. She wanted to get on friendlier terms with the woman, put aside her ridiculous feelings of jealousy. Although Alicia had made the invitation for her and a partner, she seemed to be here alone.

'Where did you and Dex meet?' Barbara asked, bringing her attention winging back.

'We worked for the same company for a while. I was secretary for the managing director at MacDales, and Dex worked in the computer department. We used to have lunch together every day…oh, there was a whole crowd of us from the office. But Dex and I usually found ourselves sitting together. We talked and talked…' She smiled, her mood suddenly wistful. 'Sometimes we were late back for work. There was no real romance at that time; we were just very good friends. Then Dex said he was leaving, starting up his own business, and I was devastated.'

'But he asked you to come and work for him?' Barbara ventured.

'Of course I did.' Dex appeared suddenly beside them. 'She was the best damned secretary in the place, and only the best is good enough for me.' He slipped a hand around her waist and pulled her close in to his side. 'I head-hunted her as soon as I had my business up and running. Isn't that right, Mrs Rowland?'

'Certainly is.' She smiled up at him. It had been exciting working with Dex, watching the business grow. She had felt a part of it.

Someone came over to claim his parents' attention and they were left alone for a moment.

'Are you OK?' Dex asked.

'Yes, of course.'

'Not getting tired or anything?' He touched her face with a gentle finger.

His concern made her heart contract sharply with love, with desire. Although she hadn't been sick throughout these early weeks of her pregnancy, she did get very tired. 'Not *that* tired,' she assured him, a teasing gleam in her eyes.

'Good. I wouldn't want the honeymoon suite I've booked to go to waste,' he said with a laugh.

'You've booked a suite here?' She looked up at him in surprise. She had thought that they were spending a quiet few days in their new home. Vicky had arranged to stay with some friends so they could have the place to themselves.

'Nope, not here.' He smiled.

'So where?'

'Don't be so impatient. It's a surprise,' he said, enjoying her curiosity.

'But I haven't organised any overnight things—all my belongings are over at our house—'

'Don't worry, everything's been taken care of…not that you need night things.' The husky, sexy drawl of his voice fired her desire.

They were interrupted by a friend of Dex's, and Alicia was left momentarily on her own. She wondered what he was planning, where they were going on honeymoon.

'Congratulations.' Maddie McDowell interrupted her thoughts and reached to kiss the air at either side of Alicia's cheeks in a theatrical show of affection.

'Thank you.' She forced herself to smile at the woman. She felt quite ashamed of herself for not being able to like her; after all she was a tremendous help to Dex.

'What do you think of your new house?' Maddie asked.

'It's wonderful.' Alicia was enthusiastic. 'Still needs a

lot of work doing to it, but it won't take long to get it right.'

Maddie's bright lips stretched in a smile. Alicia liked her suit and wide-brimmed hat; the pale colour looked fabulous against her dark colouring.

'Yes, but it's got that wonderful lounge. And the views are so lovely that they make up for any small problems inside, I'm sure,' she drawled now.

Alicia frowned. 'Have you seen the house?'

'Oh, yes.' Maddie opened wide green eyes. 'Dex asked my opinion on it before he signed on the dotted line. He wanted a woman's perspective.'

Alicia's heart jolted fiercely against her chest at this news. How could Dex do that to her? she asked herself silently. How could he ask another woman's opinion on their home and not ask *her*?

She pulled herself together sharply. 'Dex brought a lot of people out to the house before we bought it,' she lied, with what she hoped was convincing confidence in her tone. She had no idea who Dex had taken to the house; all she knew was that he hadn't taken *her*. 'It's reassuring to get a few opinions before you make such a massive purchase.'

Alicia reached for her glass of orange juice and slanted a look at Maddie. 'Dex is such a darling. He went out of his way to find the exact house that I had once described to him as one that I'd love. He's so romantic—spoils me like crazy.' Maybe she was going overboard, but she was pleased to see that the smug look had gone from Maddie's face now.

Dex returned to her side. 'What are you two so deep in conversation about?'

'Just your house, darling.' Maddie smiled at him a trifle coquettishly. 'Congratulations, by the way.' She stood on tiptoe to kiss his cheek and he placed a hand lightly at her waist.

'I know that now isn't the time to talk about business,' Maddie continued as she pulled away. 'But we are going to need the new projection figures soon.'

There followed a conversation that Alicia found hard to follow. They talked about people they had met in Perth, people Alicia hadn't a clue about. She frowned. If Dex and Maddie had to talk about business now, what had they been talking about when they had stood alone at the other side of the room? The fact that Dex had brought Maddie to look at their house fuelled suspicions that wouldn't stop nagging.

Dex reached to put his empty glass down and glanced at Alicia. She was looking out of the windows, an expression of sadness in the blue of her eyes.

He frowned and touched her arm. 'Alicia? What are you thinking about?' he asked gently.

Aware that Maddie was listening, Alicia shrugged lightly. 'Nothing very much.'

'She's dreaming about domestic bliss,' Maddie put in with a tight smile. 'Babies and keeping house.'

Peter wandered over in time to hear the woman's comment, and he looked at her with a raised eyebrow. 'I should think if Alicia is dreaming about anything it's the career she could still have as a top model in Sydney,' he enthused. 'It's only that she and Dex are so much in love, or I'm sure that's where she would be now.'

'Yes, all right, Peter.' Alicia cut across her friend as he seemed set to continue on this favourite theme of the moment. She was grateful for the morale boost, but embarrassed by his enthusiasm for a subject she didn't want to pursue. It reminded her that Dex didn't love her, had been willing to let her go before he had known she was pregnant. She glanced up at Dex. He was looking very serious.

The best man interrupted their conversation. 'Ladies and gentlemen, before the bride and groom depart for their honeymoon, I'd like you to raise your glasses and join me in wishing them every happiness for the future.'

There were cheers as the toast was made, and calls for Dex to make a speech.

Dex's manner was calm and considered as he looked at Alicia. 'I'd just like to say, on behalf of my wife and I, thank you for coming and helping to make this day so special.'

Cheers followed these words and he smiled at Alicia.

'And thank you to Alicia for saying yes. I'm a very lucky guy.' Amidst wild applause he bent and kissed Alicia.

She clung to him for a moment, her eyes closed, wishing he meant that—truly meant it from his heart.

The next moment they were being ushered outside and down to the hotel's small wooden jetty, where a speedboat waited for them. The words 'JUST MARRIED' were on a notice pinned to its sleek lines.

Alicia laughed in surprise.

As everyone crowded on to the jetty to wave them off, Alicia embraced her sister. 'Did you know about this?' she asked.

'Of course,' Vicky said with a gleam of mischief in her yes. 'Who do you think packed your honeymoon case?'

Dex had climbed down into the boat and now lifted a hand to help her down.

She had to take off her high heels and hold her long dress up as she transversed the awkward leap away from firm land. Then Dex's arms were around her, steadying her.

A cheer went up from the waiting group on the jetty. The engine roared to life and Dex turned it out towards the open sea.

As Alicia waved to her sister and friends she noticed that

Maddie stood apart from the crowd. Unlike the others, she wasn't waving. Her stillness, the expression on her face created a stir of unease in Alicia.

'Now it's just you and I,' Dex said gently against her ear.

She turned and smiled up at him, instantly forgetting the other woman.

They sped across the turquoise waves, the wind blowing through their hair, the spray of salt against their lips.

The sun was starting to go down when Dex slowed the boat and guided it slowly in towards a small palm-fringed island. The sky was streaked with a golden-red glow which lit the fluffy clouds of evening as if someone had turned on a light behind stained glass. The silky wash of the sea was tinged with its glorious vivid colours, leaving the trees silhouetted as dark shapes against the shoreline. Dex cut the engine, and there was stillness, peaceful tranquillity. Just the lapping of the ocean against the boat and the hum of the insect world broke the silence.

He allowed them to drift in as far as possible to the milky-white beach. Then he had to take off his shoes and socks and jump out to pull the boat further up the shore.

Alicia pulled her dress up and got out to help him. The water was warm against her skin, the sand scrunching wetly between her toes.

She giggled as finally they let the boat go and both sat down breathlessly on a fallen tree branch.

'What are you laughing at?' he enquired with a wry curve of his lips.

'Us. I bet we make a very strange picture.' She looked over at him in his dark wedding suit, his flower still in his buttonhole, his feet bare. 'We look as if we've been ship-wrecked from the *Titanic*.'

'Do we?' He glanced down at himself and grinned.

'Well, I do, anyway.' Then he looked back at her. 'But you look…spectacular.'

The long gold dress caught the glimmer of fading light as if someone was shining a spotlight on her. Her blonde hair was in disarray over her shoulders. She looked wildly exotic, enticing.

Something about the way he was looking at her made the amusement fade away. She felt her heart thump wildly, with need, with a desire that filled her senses entirely.

She moistened the softness of her lips with the tip of her tongue. Suddenly she felt very shy, very unsure.

'It seems a long time since we made love,' she whispered unsteadily.

He didn't say anything for a moment. Then he inclined his head. 'It's been a pretty hectic time.'

'You've seemed distant these last few weeks.'

'Have I?' He frowned. 'I didn't mean to be. I've just had a lot on my mind, one way and another.'

'Such as whether or not we're doing the right thing getting married?' she had to ask, even though deep down she wasn't sure she wanted to hear the answer.

'Of course not.' His voice was firm.

'You had no last-minute doubts this morning, then?'

His eyes moved over the softness of her skin, the vulnerable curve of her lips. 'No doubts whatsoever.' The whispered words were like a caress; they stole across her consciousness and stirred up such emotion inside her.

'It…it's just that under normal circumstances I suppose it's usual for people to have wedding nerves.' Her words came out in a rush. She was afraid to read too much into the way he was looking at her, but it was hard not to feel a tinge of hope…a flare of hunger for the love she craved. 'And I suppose as our wedding has been…arranged…with practicalities uppermost in our hearts and minds rather than…the usual emotions…' She struggled to say the word 'love', and then skipped over it, scared to voice it. 'I assumed you might have had more than the average amount of doubts this morning.'

'Did you have doubts?' His voice was so steady and controlled, so far away from the way she felt.

'I was scared,' she admitted huskily.

He reached across and touched her face. The tenderness in his eyes made her heart slam crazily against her breast. 'We'll make it work; we're good together.'

'Yes.' She looked away from him, her heart dropping. 'You're being very practical, Dex. But I have moments when I'm so unsure about everything.'

The stars were coming out, and she noticed absently how bright they were, twinkling against the dark blue of the sky. The sea had changed from its vivid, intense colours to the inky black of night, and the gentle swish of the waves against the shore was balm to her troubled thoughts.

'I don't think I've been practical at all,' he said quietly. 'I've had moments recently when I've told myself I'm a damn fool.'

She looked sharply back at him.

'I've been guilty of taking our relationship…what we have together very much for granted,' he whispered, his dark eyes intense, his mouth set in a grim line. 'You mean so much to me, Alli, and today, when I stood next to you at the altar, it was one of the most special moments of my life.' He reached and took her hand, squeezing it tightly. 'I was so happy that you had consented to be my wife, that we'll be a family together.'

'It was special for me too.' She felt a lump in her throat as she wondered if his main emphasis was on the fact that they would be a family, and her eyes prickled with tears.

'Don't cry, Alli,' he said gently.

'I'm not.'

He reached across and brushed a gentle finger under the wetness of her eye. 'You are.'

'I'm just happy.' In a way that was the truth. And at least Dex wasn't regretting their marriage. Even if she was not the grand passion of his life, he cared for her deeply, and those feelings could grow.

She glanced over at him. He was regarding her steadily, a bleak look in the darkness of his eyes.

Despite the warmth of the night a cold shiver ran through her body. 'Why are you looking at me like that?'

'Because I know you feel as if you're giving up a career opportunity in Sydney—'

'I don't feel like that.' She cut across him earnestly. 'I'm happy to be here with you.'

'But you're also thinking about what you've given up,' Dex said quietly.

She shook her head. 'That agency in Sydney was probably only interested in me because it was Peter who sent in the photographs. He's made quite a name for himself now, and he's very talented. He can make anyone look good.'

Dex laughed at that.

'What?' She looked at him, puzzled. 'What's so funny?'

'That's exactly what Peter said you would say.'

'Well, it's true.' She shrugged.

'It's not true,' Dex said quietly. 'You probably could have made it. Peter does have a professional eye. He's made a lot of money out of his career, and he knows a thing or two.'

'It's all irrelevant,' she said, wanting to forget the subject. 'They wouldn't want me now, anyway, not unless it's to model maternity wear.' She said the words lightly. She honestly didn't care about modelling; it was the last thing on her mind.

'It's not irrelevant. I'm just wondering if you're going to blame me for ruining your career in years to come,' he said slowly.

'Dex! How can you even say that?' Her voice came out in a horrified hushed tone.

'It occurred to me today at our reception. Peter was so sure when he spoke about what could have been, and there was a moment when you looked sad.'

She shook her head. 'The most important thing to me now is my baby.'

'Our baby,' he corrected her quietly. He moved so that he was sitting closer to her, then took his hand away from hers to rest it against her stomach. It was relatively flat, just the slightest soft swell to indicate the changes within her body.

'I'll do my very best for both of you. I promise you that. I want you to be happy, Alicia.'

'I know.' Her eyes moved with tenderness over his face. 'And I'll do my best for you.'

'What are we going to call him?' he asked suddenly.

'How do you know it's going to be a him?' Alicia asked with a smile.

'Male intuition,' he said firmly.

'I think it will be a little girl.' Alicia leaned her head against his shoulder and watched as the moon climbed higher in the Milky Way. 'We'll call her Katy.'

'I was thinking Clark.'

Alicia turned and looked at him. 'What, like Superman?'

He grinned. 'Why not?'

'Because I think I'm having a girl, that's why not. And anyway, even if it is a boy, I wouldn't call my son Clark.'

'OK, if it's a girl we'll call her Katy; if it's a boy we'll call him Sam…what do you say?'

She put her arms up around his neck and buried her head in against him. 'Can you hear a brass band playing somewhere, Dex?' she whispered softly. 'Because I think I've fallen in love.'

He put a hand under her chin and tipped her face up towards his. 'I'm flattered, Alli, but you don't have to pretend. I'd rather you were just honest with me,' he breathed huskily.

She stared up at him wordlessly. Of course she knew why he wouldn't accept her admission of love. Because he couldn't say it back to her. The knowledge stung painfully, but it was no surprise. 'If…that's what you want.' She managed to keep her voice steady, but it was a tremendous effort.

For a moment there was a dark, shadowed expression in his eyes. 'It's important that we're both honest with each other,' he murmured. Then he bent and kissed her lips tenderly, as if tasting them for the first time. There seemed to be a wealth of emotion in his kiss, and she responded hesitantly. The fact that she wanted to read so much more into that caress gave it a bittersweet flavour…

The kiss changed from tender to demanding and passionate within a few seconds. Hunger flared instantly to life as she felt his hands moving over her body, knowing and provocative. His mouth invaded the softness of hers with searing certainty now.

Were a few unspoken words of love so important when they could share a passion like this? she thought dazedly. Surely the chemistry and the vehement way they responded to each other spoke much louder than any words?

Then he pulled back. 'Shall we retire to our room before I make you mine right here out on the beach?' He smiled.

She nodded, and slipped her hand in his as they walked along the deserted shoreline.

The eucalyptus scent from the gum trees and the salty tang of the hot night air filled her senses. They didn't speak, just listened to the sounds of the Australian bush life. The deep clacking of the tree frogs, the hiss of the cicadas, the soft lap of the waves.

'Here we are.' He nodded towards a wooden chalet right on the edge of the beach, the only building in sight. Lanterns flickered invitingly from the porch.

'Where did you find this place?' she asked wonderingly as he led her up the steps and into the most delightful room.

The wooden floors were polished and covered with warm vivid blue rugs. Their luggage stood next to a large four-poster that was romantically draped in white muslin. The flicker of storm lanterns lit the night; there was no electricity.

'It's part of a hotel complex on the other side of the island. It's called the Honeymoon Hideaway.' Dex grinned. 'It may look quaint, but don't worry; it does have all the modern conveniences.' He opened a door through to a bathroom that had a sunken bath and a shower.

'You've thought of everything.'

'I hope so.' He smiled. 'Do you mind if I have a quick shower first?'

'No. You go ahead. I'll open my case and find out what Vicky has packed for me.'

Alicia hummed to herself as she unpacked. She still felt warmed by the heat of Dex's kisses. They had filled her with renewed confidence about this marriage.

She could hear the heavy jet of water from Dex's shower. The thought that they were alone, with no interruptions from work or other people to intrude, made her heart feel lighter than it had in ages. They would have time to talk about their feelings, plan for the future. And maybe one day Dex would tell her he loved her.

She smiled as she took out the most exquisite white silk negligee. There was a little card attached to the lingerie. And, scrawled in Vicky's writing, a message which read, 'A little gift from me to you.'

Alicia smiled. Her sister was such a romantic. She put the nightwear on the bed, and then on impulse opened Dex's case, intending to unpack for him.

There was a card on top of the neat pile of clothing, with a picture of a single red rose on its glossy surface.

Smiling, thinking it was a message of good luck from someone, she opened it. The smile fell from her lips as she read the words. And suddenly she felt as if her life had just fallen apart.

> Dearest Dex,
> I just wanted to tell you how much Perth meant to me. I know you feel the same way I do, and that those few days were incredibly precious for both of us. I understand your reasons for marrying Alicia. I wish you well, and I want you to know that I love you…I'm here for you when you need me.
>
> Maddie.

Alicia heard the shower switch off, but she couldn't move. She felt numb as she read the message over and over again.

The next moment Dex walked out into the room.

'Bathroom's all yours,' he said cheerfully.

Her eyes moved over the powerful lines of his body. He was wearing a white towelling dressing gown, nothing else. Her heart lurched. He was so handsome, even with his dark hair damp from the shower. He looked like a movie star.

It was no wonder that women…Maddie…found him irresistible.

Anger ate her up. All that talk earlier about how special she was to him, how they should be honest with each other had been nonsense…utter moonshine. He'd been stringing her along, paying lip service as far as he possibly could just to keep his baby. Their marriage was a sham and she was the biggest fool in all the world for believing he could ever want her on any emotional level.

'Alicia? He was looking at her strangely now. 'Are you OK?'

She didn't answer him, couldn't find her voice. She was too furious, too hurt.

He looked at the card that she was fingering absently as she sat. 'What's that?'

She met his eyes, and from nowhere a cold calm settled around her heart. 'It's for you.' She held it out to him. 'It was in your case.'

She watched as he took it from her and read it. Noted the deep frown on his forehead, the expression of shock in his eyes when he looked up at her. 'You don't believe this, do you?'

She flicked him a look of utter contempt.

'Alli, nothing happened between Maddie and I in Perth.' His voice was earnest and imploring.

She stood up from the bed. 'Don't insult my intelligence, Dex.'

'I'm telling you the truth.'

Her eyes collided with his and they blazed in fury. 'You wouldn't know the truth if it jumped up and bit you. You lied to me, deceived me, and I…I hate you for it.'

'Don't say that, Alicia.' Dex's face was ashen for just a moment.

'Why not? Weren't you the one who said we should be

truthful with one another?' Her voice dripped with sarcasm. She wanted to hurt him now, make him feel as low and as bad as she did.

'I haven't lied to you.' In contrast to her, he sounded calm. Only the darkness and the strain around his eyes betrayed the fact that he was holding on to control with difficulty.

'Next you'll be telling me that note is just a figment of my imagination.' She nodded towards the card he still held.

'It's a figment of Maddie's imagination,' he answered tersely. 'Nothing happened between us in Perth.'

She watched as he tore the card into small pieces that fell to the floor like confetti.

'I don't believe you.'

'It's the truth.'

'You took her out to our house.' Alicia suddenly remembered her conversation with Maddie at the reception. 'You showed her around our house before you had even taken me there.'

'Well…yes. But only because she happened to turn up just as I was heading out there one day. Said she had some important business to discuss and it wouldn't wait—'

'I bet it wouldn't.' Alicia practically spat the words out. 'What did you do? Take her in our bedroom?'

'No, of course I didn't.' He sounded angry now.

Alicia shook her head. She didn't believe him. 'You've really taken me for a fool, haven't you?' She realised there was no point kidding herself about their marriage. The reality was that he was already having an affair with Maddie. That was why he hadn't made love to her for so long. It was all so clear now. 'Well, it's not too late. We can get the marriage annulled.'

'What?' He stared at her, shocked. 'Look—'

'Save it, Dex. I don't want to hear any more of your lies.

I could have put up with a marriage without love, a marriage that contained mutual respect, friendship, all the things you have been expounding since you first talked me into this. But I won't put up with you cheating on me. That is unacceptable…reprehensible…and I won't tolerate it.'

For a moment Dex's eyes seemed to darken to deepest midnight-black. 'You don't have to.' He reached out a hand to her. 'I haven't been unfaithful to you. It isn't what you think. Yes, Maddie and I once had a relationship…a fling—'

'In Perth?'

'No. Nothing happened in Perth.'

She shrugged his hand away. 'I think you'd better go.'

'Go?' He was incredulous. 'We need to sit and discuss this calmly, Alli. You're getting it all out of proportion—'

'Am I?' She flashed him a furious look. 'You've deceived me and you think I'm getting it out of proportion? It doesn't bode well for our future, does it, Dex?' She moved away from him, snapped up her night things from the bed and headed for the bathroom. 'I'm going to have a shower now.' Her voice was weary; she needed to be alone. 'You said there was a hotel on the other side of the island. I suggest you go to it.'

She marched away from him, closing the door firmly behind her.

'You're angry, and I understand that.' Dex's voice was cool and calm from the other side.

She met her reflection in the bathroom mirror. The flicker of the candlelight played over the long romantic dress. Dex could never understand. Her wedding night, the night she had looked forward to with excitement and longing, was ruined. Her dreams lay about her like shattered pieces of glass. Sharp, painful.

She wanted to cry, but her hurt was too deep for that.

'Alicia, give me a chance to explain this to you. You owe me that at least.'

'I don't owe you anything.' She pulled at the fastenings of her dress with angry hands.

'Yes, you do. I'm your husband—'

'In name only.'

'If that's—'

She reached to turn the full force of the shower on so that his words were drowned.

She swallowed on a very hard lump in her throat. She felt helpless suddenly, and more alone than she had ever been in her life. But she'd rather be on her own than put up with Dex's infidelity.

CHAPTER SIX

WHEN Alicia returned to the bedroom a while later, it was empty. The sight of the marriage bed, the covers folded back invitingly, taunted her.

She ran a soothing hand down over the satin of her negligee. She'd done the right thing, she told herself fiercely. Yet the words felt hollow inside her.

The silence was so powerful, so lonesome that it seemed unbearable. She pushed the mosquito net back from the bed and sat down on the side.

The pieces of torn card were still on the floor from when Dex had let them drop.

How long had his affair with Maddie been going on? she asked herself, for what felt like the millionth time.

Despite the heat of the night she felt cold and numb inside.

The door opened abruptly and Dex stepped inside from the porch. He had dressed in jeans and a checked shirt, she noticed. His expression was serious, troubled. He looked how she felt, she thought wryly.

'I thought I told you to leave me alone.' She glared at him. Yet despite everything there was a small part of her that was glad he had come back.

'Come on, Alli, you didn't mean that, surely?' His voice was gentle. 'What are you trying to do? Break my heart?'

'Do you have a heart to break?' she muttered tersely.

'Yes.' His voice was very gentle, and the way he was looking at her now did strange things to her pulse.

Had she no shame, no pride? she asked herself silently,

furiously. How could she want a man who didn't love her? How could she still feel churned up with need, with love, just at the merest hint of desire in his eyes?

'Where you're concerned I do.'

She didn't answer him. He knew all the right things to say when it suited him, she told herself staunchly.

'I've done a lot of things wrong where you and I are concerned, Alli. But having an affair with Maddie is not one of them.' He came further into the room and closed the door.

'I'd like to believe that.' Her voice was just the merest whisper.

'It's the truth.' He came across and crouched down beside her, his dark eyes earnest. 'You have to believe me, Alicia.'

She lowered her gaze away from him. When he looked at her like that it was too easy to fall for any line he might care to throw at her.

'Yes, Maddie and I once had a…relationship, but it was years ago.' He put a hand under her chin as she made to turn further away from him. 'No, Alli, look at me.' He tipped her face so that she met the darkness of his eyes. 'It was while I was working at MacDales, long before you worked there. We had a brief fling; that's all you could call it. Then I discovered she was married and I finished it very quickly. I was upset to discover I'd been seeing a married woman and that she had been lying to me. I felt a fool for not realising the truth sooner. I didn't see her again for ages, then recently I met her at a computer convention in town.'

He paused, took a deep breath. 'We had a drink; she told me she was divorced. She apologised for her behaviour years ago, said that she had been very unhappy in her marriage and had needed someone.' He shrugged. 'She said she hoped what had happened between us wouldn't stop us just being friends and that she was very interested in my business plans.'

'Huh!' Alicia rolled her eyes. 'I bet she was.'

'Come on, Alli, she's a woman of the world. I honestly thought that the personal side of our involvement was long forgotten and that there was no reason why we shouldn't have a business association.'

Alicia shook her head. 'I can think of plenty of reasons why you shouldn't have gone anywhere near her.'

'In retrospect, maybe you're right. But anybody can be wise after the event, can't they?' he said calmly. 'After that first conversation all we ever talked about was business. She is a shrewd business person; she has all the right contacts. She gave me no reason to suspect that she was interested in anything else.' He frowned. 'Then in Perth, as soon as I had signed our contract, she came on to me.'

'And you took her to bed—'

'No.' He stared at her intently.

Her heart was slamming painfully against her ribs at the very thought of him holding Maddie, making love to her.

'Alicia. Nothing happened. She kissed me—'

'I wouldn't call that *nothing*.'

'Well, actually, it was pretty enlightening.' For a second there was a gleam of humour in the darkness of his eyes.

That fuelled her anger again. 'Enlightening?' She glared at him.

'I didn't want her at all, and it made me realise just how much I wanted you.' His voice was like a caress. It stilled her anger, sent her emotions into a spiral of confusion.

'Don't, Dex!' She tried to look away from him but he wouldn't let her. His fingers cupped her face with gentle insistence, keeping her eyes steady with his.

'Don't lie to me any more.' Her voice was soft and pleading.

'I'm telling you the truth.'

She wanted to believe him so much.

Her body was urging her to throw away her suspicions, yet her rational mind urged caution, kept reminding her that Dex wanted his child very much, and that he could be so devastatingly persuasive when he wanted to be.

'How did that card get into your case?' she asked him suddenly.

He hesitated. 'I don't know, but our bags were sitting in the hotel reception for a while today. She could have slipped it in then.'

She stared at him, not knowing what to think. She didn't want to be used, made a fool of. Yet at the same time she loved him, and what he was saying did sound sincere and truthful.

'Alli, please don't throw away what we've got together. Not over something as stupid as this. Maddie means nothing to me.' His thumb stroked over the trembling curve of her lips in a silky caress that made the soft skin tingle with awareness.

She tried to think straight, but it was getting more and more difficult. 'You should have told me about Maddie before.'

He nodded. 'I realise that now. But I just wanted to forget about it, concentrate on business, and I suppose I didn't want you getting the wrong idea. Forgive me, Alicia,' he breathed huskily, and leaned forward, his lips replacing the touch of his fingers on her lips in a soft yet urgent kiss.

Her fingers clenched and unclenched on the soft covers of the bed as she fought for some control, fought not to respond.

He pulled back and looked at her, anxiety darkening his

eyes even further. 'You didn't mean it when you said you hated me, did you?'

'No…' Her voice came out in a trembling sigh. 'I was just so angry…'

'And you believe me?'

'I'm just wondering what else you haven't told me,' she whispered unsteadily. 'What are the other mistakes you said you'd made?'

He smiled at that. It was a lop-sided, endearing smile that made her heart want to melt.

'I nearly let you go once, and that would have been the worst mistake of my life.' He reached forward and kissed her again.

This time she kissed him back, with the full force of her need for him.

They were both breathless as they broke apart.

'I'm sorry I didn't tell you about Maddie,' he said in a low tone.

'What are you going to do about her?' she asked, tracing a finger along his jawline, her mind preoccupied now with her desire for him.

'I'll talk to her when we get back. She'll see sense, I'm sure, especially now that I'm married. And anyway, she's an attractive woman. Quite probably she'll be seeing some-one else by the time we get back to work.'

Alicia remembered the way she had watched them as they'd left for their honeymoon and wasn't too sure about that.

Dex stroked her hair back from her face, his eyes moving over her features as if committing her to memory. 'You know, I had the most awful moment earlier today.' He spoke almost to himself.

'Why, what happened?' she asked, puzzled.

He shook his head. 'Nothing happened…it was just a feeling.'

He saw her look of perplexity and smiled sadly. 'You'll think I'm crazy…I shouldn't even mention this. It was just that the doorbell rang this morning and I thought it was my best man. Before I turned the handle I had this weird flashback to the morning when I should have married Clare.'

Alicia went still. She could hear her heart beating in her ears. Feel it heavy against her chest.

'For just a moment it was as if I was back in time. I saw my friend standing on the doorstep, the expression in his eyes as he told me the news about Clare. And as I turned the handle I suddenly thought…Oh God, don't let anything have happened to Alicia…I couldn't bear it…'

'Oh, Dex!' Her eyes filled with tears and she put her arms around him, snuggling her head against his shoulder. She knew it took a lot for Dex to talk about Clare; that he had opened up to her at all on this subject made her feel as if they had just taken a giant step forward. 'Darling, it must have been awful. But it's in the past, and—'

'I know that, Alli.' He cut across her, his voice grave. He pulled her away from him and looked deep into her eyes. 'But that happening this morning made me face something, made me realise what I hadn't consciously thought about before. Clare is the reason why I haven't been able to take a more conventional approach with our courtship.'

Alicia stared at him.

'I didn't take you house-hunting with me…I didn't take you to pick your own ring…I have been deliberately avoiding any similarity with the past. Determined that my relationship with you is different.'

She swallowed hard. 'Because you still miss Clare…because no one will ever replace her—'

'Of course no one will ever replace her.' His voice was gruff. 'She was her own unique person.'

The words cut into Alicia's soul, but she understood. After all, she knew what it was like to lose someone you loved. It did change you...it did affect you in ways that you never would have thought.

'But it wasn't that, Alli.' He stroked the side of her face, looked deep into the loveliness of her eyes. 'I was just so damn scared of history repeating itself that I've been deliberately going out of my way to ensure that things were different this time.'

'Dex...' Her voice held a wealth of emotion, of empathy and tenderness. She reached to stroke her hands through his hair. Her compassion was in her eyes, in her fingertips, there for him to take should he need it.

'I don't deserve you, Alli...' He bent his head and kissed her with brutal passion on the fullness of her lips. 'Don't deserve your understanding...your tenderness.

'Everyone deserves a second chance, Dex,' she said softly.

He smiled and kissed her. 'We'll make this marriage work, Alli,' he growled against her ear as he kissed her and then lowered his lips to her neck. 'We're good together, passionately good.'

She pulled away from him for a moment. It was strange, but in the space of a few moments the centre of her concerns had moved from Maddie to his previous fiancée. It was as if Clare's ghost was permanently with them. The idea made her shiver.

'You OK?' He frowned, as if aware that her thoughts had moved, had become shadowed by the past.

'Yes...' She wanted to forget all her doubts, just lie with him, have his arms around her, holding her, closing out the doubts.

The flicker of the candlelight played over his handsome features, the golden bronze of his skin, the powerful muscle of his chest and upper arm.

She realised suddenly that he was looking at her with equal intensity. 'You look fabulous, by the way,' he breathed, his eyes raking over her slender figure in the white negligee, a gleam of hunger in the darkness of his eyes.

Her hands curled into tight fists at her sides as she felt an answering need immediately rising inside her.

He looked from her towards the sheets on the bed behind her. 'The marriage bed awaits,' he murmured softly. 'Shall we...?'

Her heart felt as if it was turning somersaults now. Yet she sat very still, just looking at him.

He frowned. 'You are feeling OK, aren't you?' he murmured. 'I mean, if you're worried about the baby or anything, I can wait. We can make love another time.'

The concern in his voice freed her from the sudden terrible paralysis of fear.

'I'm fine.' She moved closer and kissed him, acting on instinct rather than conscious thought.

He eased her back on to the bed with a gentle movement. 'That's better,' he murmured as he moved to sit beside her.

His hand traced the soft curve of her face. The sensation sent shivery, whisper-sweet sensations tickling through her.

His finger traced down the long line of her neck. She lay perfectly still, her eyes locked with his.

His hand moved to cup her breast through the silk negligee. Her body responded immediately to the caress, tightening with need, tingling with awareness.

Her mind refused to function as his fingers toyed with

the delicate buttons that ran all the way down the front of the gown.

He unfastened all of them slowly, and then with an impatient sweep of his hands pulled the material aside, exposing her naked body to his gaze. Slowly, deliberately, he let his eyes travel down her body.

'Your breasts are fuller,' he murmured, noting the subtle changes to her body since she had become pregnant.

For a moment she felt a shiver of self-consciousness, the notion that perhaps he was comparing her figure to Clare's making her reach for her nightgown to cover herself.

He stopped her, his hands firm yet gentle over hers. 'They're beautiful, Alli. You're beautiful.' He whispered the words seductively, his eyes meeting hers with warmth, as if her embarrassment at his remark amused him.

'Dex, I...' She didn't know what she'd been going to say. But all coherent thought was torn away from her anyway as he straddled her and his hands moved to cup her naked breasts.

She gave a small gasp of pleasure as he stroked the silky texture of her skin, rubbed at the rosy areolae of her nipples with the tips of his thumbs, creating a tormenting, teasing, deliciously pleasurable sensation inside her.

He watched as her nipples hardened, strained for his caress. Then he bent his head and his lips encircled one rosy, hard peak, his tongue darting over it with wet, hot lashes of pure pleasure.

She closed her eyes at the exquisite explosion of feeling he created inside her. Her hands moved and she found herself stroking her fingers through his hair, loving the thick softness, urging him to continue.

When his mouth left one breast and moved towards the other, it was left hard with desire, heavy with longing. She moved her hand and placed it over her flesh, seeking to keep in the warmth, to satisfy the ache building and building inside her.

She shuddered with sheer bliss as his lips closed over her other nipple, sucking, kissing, tormenting her. His teeth grazed slightly over the sensitised flesh and she drew in her breath, half crazy with need now.

For a long while he continued to play with her, provoking within her a total abandonment of pride, of thought, of reason. All that remained was love, desire, and a demand by her body to have him inside her.

He pulled back from her and her eyes flew open. 'Don't stop,' she whispered.

He smiled as he saw the pleading light in her eyes, the way her body writhed slightly beneath him, ready, ripe, his for the taking.

He reached out a hand and touched the soft triangle of hair between her legs. She moaned, and bit down on her lips as he started to stroke her there.

'Please, Dex. Come inside me,' she murmured fervently.

His reply was to stroke deeper, circling, rubbing, into the sticky wet softness of her.

She moaned, touching her fingers against her breasts in an attempt to ease their throbbing need for him.

He smiled, sitting above her, watching her movements with a lazy gleam of approval in the dark depths of his eyes.

Then he started to unbutton his shirt, unfasten the buckle of his jeans.

Her senses reeled. She wanted him so much.

'Hell, Alli, you're fabulous in bed,' he murmured, his tone taunting, teasing. 'So abandoned, so wanton...'

She felt a hot flush in her cheeks at those words. Her hands dropped from her breasts, her body stilled.

He smiled and reached for her hands, to replace them

back on her body. 'Don't stop,' he told her huskily. 'I adore it.'

He bent and kissed her on the lips, a sensational, erotic kiss. And while he was kissing her his body moved gently, possessively into hers.

It was raining. One of those torrential tropical downpours as if God was throwing buckets of water out of the heavens.

Alicia lay awake, listening to the pounding of the water against the roof, staring into the darkness of the room.

Dex was asleep beside her, his passion spent, his arm loosely resting against her waist.

Their lovemaking had been incredible. But then they had always been sexually compatible. What was it Dex had said earlier? 'Don't stop, I adore it.' Not, I adore *you*...I love *you*.

Whereas she loved and adored him. She tried to close her mind to such thoughts but they wouldn't go away. She wondered if for him it was just 'good sex.' It was all very well telling her how important she was to him, but *why* was she important? Because she was the mother of his child?

A flash of lightning illuminated the bedroom. It seemed to flash inside Alicia's head.

Suddenly she was remembering something Dex's mother had said at the reception. 'Even when he eventually started to date again all the girls he was drawn to looked a bit like Clare,' she had said. 'Dark hair, green eyes. It was as if subconsciously he was searching for her.'

Maddie had dark hair and green eyes. The connection made her feel sick suddenly.

Was that the reason he had been attracted to Maddie? Had indulged in an affair with her once? And, if so, what was to stop those feelings surfacing every time he looked at the woman? He wasn't fully over Clare; that much was obvious from what he had said tonight.

She looked across at him. His lashes were long and dark against his skin. Sleep made him look more vulnerable. The calm, confident way he held his head, met her eyes, was hidden.

He doesn't really love you... The words mocked her. He wants the baby, so he's made a commitment. But you'll always be second best to the way he felt about Clare.

No matter how Dex wrapped it up, with flowery sentiment about how important she was and how special, this was a marriage of convenience.

She was married to a man who not only didn't love her, but was probably sexually attracted to someone else. She believed that nothing had happened between him and Maddie in Perth...she had to believe that otherwise everything in her life was a lie. But as for the fact that he hadn't wanted Maddie when she kissed him...that was another story.

Dex rolled over and his hand moved away from her waist. Alicia took the opportunity to pull back the covers and climb silently out of bed.

She put on her dressing gown and stood at the window, looking out. The rain had stopped as abruptly as it had started. The sun was starting to come up over the sea in a pink haze, its first watery rays catching the raindrops that glittered on the lush greenery.

On impulse Alicia opened the door and stepped out from the air-conditioned cool of the room into the steamy heat of the morning.

The wooden veranda was warm and wet beneath her bare feet. The air was alive with the sound of birds. She watched a white cockatoo swoop and land on the branch of a banana tree.

The sea rippled in against the shore, its surface a glassy mirror of the opalescent sky.

She could take the boat and leave. The idea came from nowhere. She could go back to her apartment and tell her landlord she had made a mistake giving in her notice. Tell Dex that she had made a mistake marrying him.

The door opened behind her and Dex came out to join her. He looked sleepy and sexily dishevelled, wearing nothing but a pair of shorts.

'What are you doing up so early?' He yawned and raked a hand through hair that was already ruffled from sleep.

'Just thinking.' Her voice felt unnaturally thick with sudden fierce emotion. How could she contemplate leaving this man when she loved him so much?

'Come and think back in bed.' He grinned, and put out a hand to draw her close in against his chest.

She rested her head against the softness of his skin, breathed in the clean male scent of him.

'What were you thinking about anyway?'

'Just wondering how long we could stay here in paradise and keep reality shut away.' It wasn't really a lie, it was what she was thinking now. When he held her in his arms she just wanted time to stand still.

'We've got two whole days.' She could hear the smile in his voice. 'Let's go back to bed and make the most of them, shall we?'

'Good idea.' She smiled.

She pushed the shadows of doubt out of her mind once and for all. Dex had said he wanted to make their marriage work and that was what was important, she decided fiercely. One day he would turn around and tell her he loved her.

CHAPTER SEVEN

It was strange leaving the house every morning with Dex. In some ways they were like a family. They dropped Vicky at school and talked about what they were going to have for dinner in the evening. Then they would get to the office and once more Dex was the boss, she was his secretary, and really it was as if nothing had changed.

They had been home from their honeymoon six weeks, and although Dex was working harder than ever things had settled down at the office. A calm seemed to have descended. Maddie was nowhere in sight.

Dex had told her that he had spoken to her about the card and she had apologised and felt bad. He said the matter was now forgotten. Alicia allowed happier thoughts to occupy her mind. She planned for their baby.

Although she was only seventeen weeks pregnant she couldn't resist buying just a few items of baby clothing in her lunch-hour, amongst them the tiniest pair of little yellow booties. She'd put them in a drawer in her office desk, not wanting to tempt fate by bringing them home. Next to them she put the gift she had bought for Dex's birthday, which was next month.

She had splashed out and bought him an expensive pair of gold cuff-links. They were more than she could afford, but she wanted to treat her husband. Dex hadn't bought himself anything for ages. He would never admit it, and he continually played down the seriousness of his financial situation, but she knew he was financially stretched to the limit, with all his money riding on the new computer game he had designed.

Dex came out of his office just as she had finished putting her shopping away.

'What are you doing?' he asked nonchalantly, leaning across the desk.

'Nothing much.' She pushed the drawer tightly closed.

'Did you send that letter to my accountant?'

'Yes, it went first thing this morning.' Alicia reached across to the papers beside her and handed him a sheet. 'I've made a copy for our files.'

'Thanks.' His eyes moved over the letter and he nodded with satisfaction.

He watched as she consulted the diary on her desk. She'd left her hair loose this morning, he noted. He liked it like that. She looked the picture of health, her skin slightly tanned, her eyes wide and bright.

Despite the fact that he had been working so hard these last weeks, they had been the happiest of his life. Being with Alicia, going with her to the hospital for the baby scan, planning for the future with optimism. Somehow it gave added purpose to work, new meaning to everything.

'You've got a meeting with the bank manager at two,' she said. 'Oh, and Robert Vaughn from the advertising agency David and Davis at four-thirty.'

She looked up at him and he smiled. 'Have I told you? Not only are you a perfect wife, you're also a damn efficient secretary,' he drawled lazily. 'I don't know how I managed to hit so lucky.'

'Dex, you're a real smoothie.' She grinned and reached for the stack of mail at the other side of her computer.

'What's that?' He nodded to a letter she had put to one side.

'That's for me,' Alicia said lightly. 'It's from that modelling agency in Sydney. They wrote to Peter again, asking if I was going to go down and see them. I don't think they can believe I'm turning them down. Peter was saying yesterday that most girls would sell their soul for the opportunity to get in with such a top agency.'

'He's probably right.'

Something about the note in his voice made her look up at him sharply. He looked tired, she thought suddenly, noticing the lines of strain around his eyes. He had been driving himself too hard this last week.

'Why don't I ring and cancel Robert?' she suggested suddenly. 'We could finish early. I'll cook us a romantic meal and you can sit and relax.'

One dark eyebrow lifted and he smiled tenderly at her. 'Thanks for the offer, Alli. It sounds wonderful, but totally impossible. I need to see Robert today so I can get the advertising campaign under way as soon as possible. I'm going to have to work even later tonight, if anything.'

Alicia frowned. Dex had been coming back to the office in the evening a lot this week. 'You need to slow down a little,' she said quietly. 'You can't keep pushing yourself like this, Dex.'

'I'll slow down as soon as this deal is up and running.' He perched himself on the edge of her desk and looked down at her. 'But I did like the sound of the romantic dinner,' he said gently. 'Shall we defer it until tomorrow night? I'll take you out somewhere glamorous and trendy.'

'You mean you don't fancy my cooking?' She slanted teasing blue eyes up at him. 'A girl could be mortally hurt, you know.'

He smiled. 'I fancy everything about you,' he assured her huskily. He reached out a finger and traced it softly, caressingly down over the smoothness of her cheek. His touch made her go warm inside, made her want to stand up and move into the circle of his arms. 'And you're an excellent cook. But you're also young and gorgeous and you should be out having fun. I want to take you somewhere special, show you off, give you a good time.'

'You're being very complimentary today. If we weren't married, Mr Rowland, I'd think you were after my body,' she said, a tantalising gleam of devilment in her eyes.

'Now you come to mention it…' He leaned forward and reached to kiss her. Their lips had barely met in a soft, sweet caress when the shrill ring of the phone interrupted them.

'Back to reality,' Alicia said reluctantly. 'But I'll look forward to tomorrow night. Not somewhere too trendy, though, Dex. I've nothing to wear.'

'Haven't you?' He frowned.

She patted her stomach and grinned. 'You may be too polite to notice, but I've put on a few pounds recently.'

She reached to answer the phone, her mood gloriously happy.

'Hey, look at this!'

Vicky's excited call greeted Alicia as soon as she stepped through the front door that evening.

'What?' Alicia followed the sound of her sister's voice through to the master bedroom.

'This.' Victoria turned around and spread her hands.

Alicia's bedroom was draped with clothes in plastic wrappers. They hung from the wardrobe doors and sat over the bed and dressing table stool.

'Where have all these come from?' Alicia asked, stunned, fingering a long black and white dress with shoe-string straps.

'That exclusive boutique in town!' Vicky's eyes were practically popping with excitement. 'A van drew up just a few minutes before you, and the lady driving it said that a Mr Rowland had asked her to drop off a selection of dresses for you to try on. She said she would pick up the garments you didn't want early in the morning.'

'S'truth! That boutique is hellish expensive!'

'I know, isn't it wonderful? Dex is such a sweetheart.' Vicky cleared a space for herself on the bed and sat down, a look of anticipation on her face. 'Well…which are you going to try on first?'

Alicia was extremely tempted. She glanced around at the beautiful array of clothing, noting that even matching accessories had been brought. Then she let her breath out on a sigh. 'None of them…they're too expensive, Vicky.' Especially as they would probably only fit her for a short duration in her present condition, she thought wryly. 'Dex can't afford to be this generous.'

'Who says?' Dex's voice coming from the doorway startled them both. 'I think that's for me to decide, and I want you to have some new things.'

'Dex, I thought you said you wouldn't be home for ages.' Alicia swung around, delighted to see him.

'I'm not home…I'm just passing through.' He grinned. 'Thought I'd check if the dresses had arrived.'

'It's really kind of you, Dex, but—'

'It isn't kind at all. You deserve to have nice clothes. Select a few, and one for Vicky.'

Victoria squealed with delight and got up from the bed to start looking through the clothes.

'Dex—'

'I've got to go, Alli.' Dex glanced at his watch. 'I've left Robert waiting for me back at the office. Look, don't wait up for me. I've got a feeling it's going to be a late session tonight, we've loads to discuss.'

'What about dinner?' She turned to walk with him to the front door.

'I'll grab something in town.'

'OK.' Alicia stood on tiptoe to kiss him on the lips. 'Thank you for the clothes,' she whispered.

He looked deep into her eyes with tender indulgence. 'I had an ulterior motive,' he murmured huskily. 'I get to see you in them.'

With a grin, he swung away from her and strode out to his car.

'What do you think?' Vicky asked a few moments later, when she walked back into the bedroom.

Alicia had to laugh. Her sister was already wearing a bright blue dress. 'You look sensational.'

'Good, because it's the only dress that will fit…the shop has sent a lot of larger sizes. Dex mustn't have known what size you are.'

'Either that or he's reckoning on me putting on another few pounds very soon.'

'Oh?' Vicky looked puzzled for a moment as she watched Alicia pull at the loose-fitting silky top she wore so that it was stretched tight around her stomach.

'Notice anything different?' Alicia asked, and grinned as Vicky's cheeks blushed a scarlet red.

'You're not!'

'I am.'

'Oh, sis.' Vicky ran to throw her arms around her. 'How wonderful!'

'We should do this more often,' Dex said as he studied his wife across the table. She was wearing her hair up, and candlelight flickered over the creamy perfection of her skin, catching the brightness of her eyes, the gleam of gold at her neck and wrists. She was wearing one of the dresses from the selection the shop had sent yesterday and she looked wonderful in it, he thought.

'It's certainly been fun,' Alicia agreed. She glanced around. The Thai restaurant was one of the most trendy places to be seen these days. Although this was Alicia's first visit she had heard how good the food was and she had not been disappointed.

'Maybe I'll take you to Thailand one day,' Dex murmured. 'You'd love it. It's a fabulous country.'

'I didn't know you'd been.' Alicia looked across at him.

He was wearing a light-coloured suit which sat well on his broad frame. He was almost too handsome, Alli thought, feeling a flutter of awareness as she met his eyes.

'Yes, a brief holiday when I was a student.'

'With Clare?' she asked, immediately curious.

He nodded. 'We went to Phuket.' He frowned.

Immediately Alicia regretted the question. Dex had seemed so happy and relaxed throughout their meal. She didn't want to spoil things.

'But that feels like another lifetime ago,' Dex said firmly, before she could change the subject. 'I'd really like to go back, show you the temples, the white palm-fringed beaches.'

'Sounds romantic,' Alicia murmured, then impulsively asked, 'Do you still think about her, Dex?'

Dex shrugged, then smiled easily across at her. 'Clare is the past. I have more important things on my mind these days…you and my baby.'

Alicia smiled back at him.

Dex reached across and touched her hand. He didn't say anything for a while, just looked deep into her eyes. 'I'm sorry I've—'

Whatever he was about to say was interrupted by a woman's voice.

'Dex…Alicia, what a delightful surprise.'

They looked up.

Maddie McDowell stood next to their table. She wore a long white dress which was very dramatic against her dark colouring. She wasn't alone; a man stood beside her. He looked to be in his late twenties, and was very handsome.

'Hello, Maddie.' Dex stood up politely.

Maddie's lips curved in a smile of pleasure. 'You haven't met John Monroe, have you? He's a dear friend.'

'No, I don't believe I've had the pleasure.' Dex stretched out a hand to the other man as Maddie made the introductions.

'Well, we'll leave you to finish your meal,' Maddie said, as Alicia also shook hands with the man. As they turned away Maddie held back, as if she had just remembered something. 'Oh, Dex, sorry to bring work up. But I left those new figures you gave me on your desk last week. I could do with looking through them again. Will you drop them over some time?'

'I'll put them in the post for you.'

'Fine. Oh, and have you mentioned my party to Alli?' Maddie looked over at her. 'Friday week…it's mostly to do with business. A few people who have expressed an interest in the computer game will be there and I think it will be good for Dex…good for all of us.'

'I see,' Alicia said coolly. 'I'll have to check the diary— see if we're free.'

Maddie nodded and strolled away to join her dinner companion at a table on the far side of the room.

'You didn't tell me that you'd seen Maddie again.' Alicia tried to keep her voice perfectly level. She didn't want to overreact. She knew Dex was doing business with the woman.

'She popped in one afternoon after you'd gone home. It

was a brief visit, just to bring herself up to date on the advertising deal, etcetera. I forgot about the damn party,' he muttered. 'We don't have to attend if you'd rather not.'

'If you think it will be beneficial for the business then of course I'll come with you.'

'It might be.' Dex sounded cautious. 'But you never know about these things.'

Alicia glanced across at Maddie and her companion. The man was gazing into Maddie's eyes with rapt attention.

'Seems she has a new love interest in her life,' Dex remarked, his voice quiet, thoughtful.

Alicia glanced back at her husband. His eyes were on the other table, but it was hard to decipher his expression. Was he jealous? she wondered suddenly, and felt a curl of apprehension at the thought. Maddie did look stunning…

Dex looked back at her and grinned suddenly. 'Thank heavens. Glad she's out of my hair.'

Alicia felt the tension leaving her body and grinned back at him.

'Shall we go?' he asked.

She nodded, and he called for the bill.

'It's been a lovely evening,' she said as they got up from the table.

'It sure has.' He put an arm around her shoulder and held her close, possessively against his side as they left. 'But I reckon the best bit is yet to come,' he murmured softly against her ear, tickling the sensitive skin and sending darts of pleasure through her body.

Dex was silent on the way home. He couldn't help wondering if Maddie was really interested in that guy she'd been with tonight. He had a notion that she was playing games. He wasn't comfortable with her party invitation either, yet businesswise it could be a good idea.

He parked the car and they walked up to the house. 'You're very quiet,' Alicia said softly.

'Sorry, I was miles away…thinking about damn work.'

'You've been putting in too many long hours.'

'Things should get easier soon.'

The night air was hot and clammy. The sounds of the insects and the gentle swish of the waves against the beach were soothing.

'I hope so.' Alicia watched as he opened the front door. The house was in darkness because Vicky was spending the night at a girlfriend's house.

'It will; trust me. In fact, I think I'll be able to do without you in the afternoons at the office over the next few weeks.' Dex flicked the lights on.

'Trying to get rid of me?' she joked.

'Of course not. But I think you should start taking it easier.'

'I'm fine, Dex, really. I don't need to take things easy.'

'I think you do. Hell, it's hot in here.' Dex walked across and flicked the air-conditioning. 'Must have switched it off by mistake,' he murmured.

He went across to the sideboard and poured himself a whisky.

'I think maybe I'll go and have a cool shower,' Alicia said quietly, watching as Dex topped up the glass. She frowned. It was unusual for Dex to drink in the house.

'Fine.' He didn't look up; he was flicking through some paperwork that he had brought back from the office.

Alicia turned away and went through to her bedroom.

She found herself thinking about Maddie.

She had felt enormously relieved, seeing her with another man…and Dex had said he was glad.

She stripped and stepped into the shower, turning the full force of the water over her.

So why had he been so quiet and withdrawn on the way home?

She turned her face up to the cleansing forceful jet of water. It felt wonderful, gushing, regenerating. She allowed it to wash over her in pounding currents, chasing away negative thoughts.

The soft click of the shower door opening made her blink.

She saw Dex step in beside her through a watery haze. His broad chest, powerful arms and wonderful physique pressed close against her, naked skin touching naked skin.

'I thought you were doing paperwork.' She gulped for air as his lips crushed against hers.

'To hell with work,' he growled against her ear. He pressed closer and she felt the cold tiles of the shower against her back and the hot demands of his body against her front.

The heavy hiss of the shower was all the sound between them as his fingers traced the firm lines of her body, finding her pleasure points and playing with her, tormenting until she was gasping for more than air.

CHAPTER EIGHT

TRUE to his word Dex cut Alicia's hours at work. She went home early each afternoon for the next couple of weeks. But whereas her workload was slacking off, Dex's seemed to be increasing. He was working later each evening. Sometimes not returning until nearly midnight.

Alicia offered to work late with him, but he wouldn't hear of it. 'I don't mind putting in these hours, Alli,' he said cheerfully, then kissed her. 'Only drawback is I'm neglecting you... Tell you what, we'll drive up to Daintree at the weekend, go walking hand in hand, just you and I...OK?'

The thought cheered Alicia as she got ready for Maddie's party on Friday night.

'Vicky, is that you?' she called out as she heard footsteps in the corridor.

Vicky popped her head around the door.

'What do you think of this dress?' Alicia gave a twirl and turned to face her sister.

'I think you look terrific,' Vicky said with enthusiasm.

The long red dress certainly did suit Alicia. It was very cleverly cut and it hid her pregnancy well. She had put her hair up in an elaborate and sophisticated style and she looked tall and slender, the shoestring straps and low front of her dress emphasising the soft golden glow of her skin.

'Would you notice that I've put on weight?' Alicia asked her cautiously.

'Just a bit.' Vicky grinned. 'Mind you, after the afternoon we've had, you've probably lost a few pounds.'

110

Vicky had helped her with some housework, and then in a fit of energetic enthusiasm they had painted the spare box room together.

It had been fun, and they had done a lot of talking and laughing. Vicky was at a loose end now school had broken up and the summer holidays stretched before her.

The shrill ring of the telephone in the hallway sent Vicky hurrying off to answer it.

She came back after a few minutes and stuck her head around the door. 'I'm going over to Jenny's house. A group of girls will be there. We're going to have a bit of a party and a sleepover to celebrate the end of our exams.'

'OK, Dex and I will drop you off on our way out,' Alicia offered.

'No…Jen's picking me up. I'm going to take my swimwear with me because we're going snorkelling in the morning.'

'So I won't see you until tomorrow afternoon, then?' Alicia said with a shake of her head.

'Something like that.' Vicky grinned.

'Well, you deserve to relax after all the hard work you've put in.'

'Thanks, sis.'

Alicia smiled to herself. It was lovely seeing Vicky so happy. She really loved living here with them. But then Dex had been wonderful with her, had made her feel warmly welcome and at home. It was something she loved him even more for.

Alicia was alone in the house when Dex arrived back from work.

'I was starting to wonder if you'd forgotten that we were going to a party tonight,' she said with a smile as he walked into the bedroom.

'Sorry, I got held up by a couple of phone calls.' His

eyes moved over her as she stood up from the dressing table. 'You look lovely,' he said gently.

'Thank you.'

She reached up to kiss him. 'Are you still managing OK without me at the office?'

'I'm managing.' He turned away from her and took off his tie. 'I see the decorator has finally been to paint the small room. About time too. Did you write him a cheque?'

Alicia didn't answer for a moment.

'Alli?' He turned and looked at her with questioning eyes.

'Actually, he didn't come,' Alicia admitted with a shrug. 'Vicky and I gave the room a lick of paint this afternoon.'

'You did what?' Dex stared at her in disbelief. 'I'm giving you time off so you can rest!'

'I know, and I did have a lie-down. But then I felt a lot better and Vicky came in and said she'd give me a hand—'

'So you thought you'd go up and down ladders for an afternoon.' Dex's voice was now very, very angry. 'Risking an accident, risking our baby.'

'Oh, come on, Dex. I didn't ''go up and down ladders.'' Vicky did the top bits. It's just a small box room; you talk as if I've been painting the Sistine Chapel.'

'It doesn't matter. You shouldn't have done it. I had organised a decorator.'

'Yes, but…' She was about to say that a decorator cost money, and he had already splashed out enough on all those clothes. She stopped herself, remembering that Dex's male pride hated it when she reminded him of their money problems. 'I was bored, if you must know…' she said instead. 'I wanted to do something energetic.'

'Bored!' he muttered with fierce intensity. 'You've given up everything for that baby…and now you're risking it all because of a moment's whim.'

'I didn't risk anything,' Alicia said, her voice unsteady now.

'Don't ever...*ever* do that again.' He turned away from her and went into the bathroom, closing the door behind him with an ominous thud.

Damn! He ran a hand through his hair, immediately annoyed with himself for snapping at her. He felt tense about this party, and hearing her say that she was bored had sent a shiver of apprehension through him.

Was she wishing she was in Sydney, having an exciting, glamorous life, instead of being stuck here with him? He wouldn't blame her. She was so young, and things weren't easy at the moment.

Maddie's house was like something from a film set. Electric gates opened into a courtyard with a fountain and the modern split-level house backed out on to a terrace with a swimming pool. Garden lanterns and underwater lights from the pool lit up the velvet darkness of the night.

A chef was sizzling large steaks on a barbecue, and tables were laid out so that guests could dine outside by the pool.

There had to be about forty or fifty guests mingling on the terrace, and a waiter circulating with drinks.

Alicia had lost Dex amidst the crowd. One moment he had been by her side, the next he was gone. Her eyes moved around the various groups of people, searching him out. She was only half listening to the couple who stood next to her, talking about the latest in computer technology.

'Of course, this new design of Dex's is totally brilliant,' the man was saying. 'Have you worked on it with him?' he asked Alicia suddenly.

'Well, I'm his secretary, so you could say that I have.' Alicia smiled politely.

'It's going to make him a very wealthy man.'

So what? Alicia felt like saying. All she wanted was Dex to love her... Her hands clenched tightly at her sides as she remembered their earlier heated exchange. He had looked at her as if he despised her, and all she had tried to do was help. She hadn't taken any risks painting that room; the idea was absurd. Yet Dex had hardly spoken to her on the way here. He had been lost in thought.

'Those gorgeous good looks and money as well,' the man's wife purred. 'He's quite a catch.'

'Don't get too excited; he's married,' her husband informed her. 'His wife is quite-stunning looking.'

Alicia frowned, and her attention swung back to them.

'That's his wife over there.' The man nodded his head to the far side of the patio.

Alicia followed their gaze, and through a parting in the crowds saw Dex talking with Maddie. They were standing very close to each other. Maddie looked fabulous in an off-the-shoulder dress, its simple lines showing the curvaceous perfection of her body, her dark hair gleaming in the soft lamplight.

'That's not his wife,' Alicia corrected them quickly.

'Are you sure?' The man frowned. 'I mean I don't know Maddie that well, she's just a business acquaintance, but I saw her having dinner with Dex a few nights ago, and she introduced him to me as her partner.'

Alicia couldn't speak for a moment, she was so surprised. 'You must be mistaken,' she said finally.

'No...that was when they invited me here. It was only...let's see...Monday last week that I went to Romanio's restaurant.'

That would have been just a couple of days after the evening Dex had taken her to the Thai restaurant. But

Maddie was seeing someone else, she reasoned... What was it Dex had said? 'Glad she's out of my hair...'

But had he meant it? a small voice asked fiercely. He had been very quiet, very thoughtful on the way home. She remembered the way he had headed for a stiff drink as soon as they'd got in. How he had followed her into the shower, made passionate love to her with a hunger that had taken her breath away. The sweet sensations that had flowed between them were now tainted with suspicion. Had his thoughts been on Maddie as he'd held her... was that what had fired his appetite?

The idea made her fists clench tightly at her sides.

If Maddie was dating another man, where was he? she wondered suddenly, her eyes scanning the crowd for a glimpse of the handsome man she had seen in the restaurant. There was no sign of him.

She looked back towards the French doors, but Maddie and Dex had disappeared inside. She saw them walking away from the crowds through the house.

'Excuse me.' Alicia moved away from the couple, who were in the middle of telling her how interested they were in Dex's next project.

It was cool inside the house, cool and silent. There was no sign of Maddie or Dex in the kitchen, or the lounge. She walked further down the corridor and could hear their voices.

'Where's the boyfriend tonight?' Dex was asking, a sardonic edge to his voice.

'I think John has served his purpose, don't you?' Maddie gave a low, melodic laugh. 'He's put dear wifey's mind at rest.'

'Maddie, I—'

'And it's made you take a look at your priorities,' Maddie continued firmly. 'I think it's time you told her that you need me, Dex.' Maddie's voice was clear, and husky with inducement. 'All this running around behind her back is driving me crazy.'

Dex's voice was low and filled with emotion. 'Yes, I need you, but—'

'But you want everything.' Maddie sounded fierce. 'Nobody can have everything, Dex.'

The door was ajar and Alicia gave it a little push, her hand trembling, her breath sticking in her throat.

The lighting was subdued in the book-lined office. Maddie was standing next to a leather-topped desk, her arms reaching up towards Dex, her eyes locked on his face. They were so engrossed in each other that they didn't hear her; they didn't look round.

'You want your baby, that's why you married her, but you don't love her; you can't even say the words,' Maddie breathed. 'Look, once the money comes flooding in you can come to some arrangement about the child, give Alli whatever she wants and take your freedom.'

Alicia backed away, her heart hammering so heavily inside her body that it was painful.

She found the bathroom, closed the door and leaned back against it. Then she stood, trying to think, but all she wanted to do was cry. Cry so hard that she couldn't think about anything except the dreadful mess that she was in.

'You don't love her; you can't even say the words.' The sentence went over and over in her mind. Maddie was so right. And Dex had told Maddie that he needed her, had said it almost fiercely.

How long had the affair been going on? He had certainly been lying to her over these last couple of weeks. And he had taken Maddie for dinner to the restaurant where he had proposed to her. All those nights when he had told her he was working late...grabbing something to eat in town…now they all took on a new slant. Suddenly she felt sick.

After a while she went to the basin and rinsed her face, then carefully tried to repair the damage to her make-up. Her skin was very pale, her eyes like huge hollows in her face.

Her worst fears were realised, she acknowledged silently as she looked at herself in the mirror. She had been fooling herself, when really she had known the truth right from the first day of her marriage.

OK, so now she had to make a plan of action, she told herself calmly. All Dex wanted from her was his baby; he didn't need her. She had to face up to that. And as that was the case she didn't need him.

She had all her emotions tightly under control when she went back out to the party.

It was hot outside, and the warmth of the night air brought some colour back to her cheeks. She took a glass of sparkling water from a tray of a passing waiter, then went to stand at the far end of the patio where it was quieter.

Dex had rejoined the party. She saw him talking to some people she didn't know. Maddie was nowhere in sight.

He looked up and caught her eyes. She watched as he smiled at the people around him, extricated himself and made his way across to her.

'I was wondering where you had got to,' he said lightly.

She didn't answer him, couldn't bring herself to look him in the eye.

'Have you had something to eat?'

No doubt he was worrying about his baby, she thought, with a wrench of feeling so deep, so painful, she couldn't bear it.

'Alli?'

'Yes...I've eaten.' She held on to her composure with extreme difficulty.

'Would you like to dance?' He indicated the patio at the far side of the house, where soft music was playing and a few couples were dancing, their arms entwined around their partners in a romantic smooch. The very thought of being so close to him made her skin tingle, made her blood race through her veins.

'I don't think so...thanks, anyway.'

His eyes moved over her, noting the shadows in the beauty of her deep blue eyes.

'Are you still angry with me for snapping at you over the decorating?'

When she didn't answer him immediately he frowned. 'Alli, I was just concerned about you—'

'About the baby,' she corrected him, her tone brusque.

'Well...yes.' He frowned. 'You shouldn't have done the damn painting...I know money is a bit tight now, but things are going to get better.'

'Are they?' There was a bitterness in Alicia's tone that had never been there before. She couldn't envisage things getting any better, and she wasn't thinking about money.

'Of course they are.' His eyes raked over the pallor of her skin. 'You still believe in me, don't you?'

She didn't answer him.

She saw the expression of hurt in his eyes, saw the way his jaw tightened, and for a moment she wanted to put her arms around him and tell him that she didn't care about anything except having his love. Then she reminded herself of how he'd lied to her...how he had been alone with Maddie this very evening, telling her how much he needed her.

'In a few months things are going to be a hell of a lot

better,' Dex told her, his voice very low, his eyes dark and intense.

She glanced at her watch. 'I'm suddenly very tired,' she said tightly.

'I've just got some business to finish up here.' Dex nodded across, towards the couple she had been speaking to earlier. 'I want to talk to Grant Hay and his wife. It shouldn't take too long.'

'I'll get a taxi.' Alicia had no intention of standing around here waiting for him a moment longer.

'Are you feeling all right?' There was immediate concern in his voice.

'Never better.' Her voice was hard. 'But I'm tired, and I'm bored, and I just want to get out of here.'

Dex frowned. 'OK, I'll come with you.'

'Don't bother.' Alicia's voice was flat. 'You get on with your business; I'd rather be alone for a while.'

Dex hesitated, then he reached into his pocket and brought out the car keys. 'If that's what you want, take the car. I'll follow in a taxi as soon as I've finished.'

Without a word she took the keys from his outstretched hand.

For a moment he watched her move away through the crowds, a worried look in his eyes, then he turned his attention to the business he wanted to discuss with Grant. He'd sort things out with Alicia when he got home.

'Not going, are you?' Maddie came through to the hall just as she was about to open the front door.

'Looks like it,' Alicia said without turning. Her heart was beating so loudly inside her body it felt painful.

'It wasn't something I said, was it?' The amusement in Maddie's voice caused a blinding flash of fury to explode inside her.

She turned then, and looked at the woman, really looked

at her, as if she were some insect that had crawled from beneath a stone. 'Keep your claws away from my husband,' she warned in a low tone.

Maddie's eyebrows rose, but her voice was perfectly cool as she replied, 'I don't know what you mean.'

'Don't give me that,' Alicia accused steadily. 'I saw you with Dex tonight. Arms wrapped around each other in a cosy scene of seduction.'

'Maybe you should be saying this to Dex, not me,' Maddie replied. 'He's the one who can't keep his hands off me.' She watched the hot flush of colour rise in Alicia's face with a look of triumph. 'I'm sorry, Alicia.'

'You don't look sorry.'

Maddie shrugged. 'Believe it or not, I didn't set out to hurt you. And I know Dex didn't either. He'll be dismayed that you've found us out. He's most insistent that nothing should upset you.'

'It's a bit late for that,' Alicia muttered, with distaste. 'How long have you been sleeping with him?'

'Come on, Alicia. You can't expect me to answer that.'

Alicia stared at her, furious, hurt, a million emotions tearing her apart. 'He told me all about the fling he had with you years ago, you know,' she said bluntly. 'He said it meant nothing, that *you* meant nothing.' Alicia watched the flash of fury in the other woman's eyes and felt a certain amount of satisfaction.

Maddie bit down on her lip. 'Yes, that's right. We enjoyed our time together years ago, but it was never serious. Then we met up again and we realised just how *much* we'd enjoyed each other…how good we had been together. When we were celebrating signing our business agreement in Perth, he kissed me, and…well, it was magical.'

'For you, maybe.' Alicia's voice was flat. 'He told me you threw yourself at him and he could only think of me.'

Maddie's eyes narrowed, she looked furious. Then abruptly she laughed. 'He's priceless, isn't he? He told me he only feels sorry for you. That he would never have married you if you hadn't been pregnant.'

Alicia felt her blood pounding through her veins in hot, angry waves. 'Well whatever he says, you're fooling yourself if you think you are in any way special. Maybe he's led you on, but all you are is a distraction, a bit on the side.'

'I don't care,' Maddie said calmly. 'I'm not looking for commitment…I've had that once and it was very boring. Dex is a very passionate, hot-blooded man…we're just enjoying ourselves. Personally, I think he's a lot like me…he's not the settling down type.' Maddie put her hand on her hip. 'If you want some advice, Alli, I'd stay quiet, allow our affair to run its course. That way maybe, if you're lucky, you'll get to keep him.'

Alicia couldn't help but laugh at the sheer audacity of that remark. 'You've got some nerve, Maddie.' She put her hand on her hip in a mocking parody of the other woman. 'And if I don't choose to take your advice?'

'You run the risk of losing everything.'

'What do you mean, everything?'

'Well, Dex could decide to just leave you and move in with me.'

'He won't do that. I'm expecting his child—'

'Yes, and he wants this baby rather badly, doesn't he?' Maddie drawled. 'But here's another scenario. You give Dex an ultimatum; finish with me, or lose his baby. Which will he take?'

'Our baby.' Alicia's voice was steady, very confident now. She knew how much Dex wanted this child.

'Maybe you're right.' Maddie nodded. 'But then I'm afraid I'd have to withdraw from our business deal.'

'You can't…you've signed an agreement, haven't you?'

'Oh, yes.' Maddie was matter-of-fact. 'I'll lose a lot of money, but then I can afford the loss…Dex can't. His business will go bankrupt.'

'You wouldn't do that,' Alicia murmured. 'It's outrageous.'

'Yes, it is, isn't it?' Maddie smiled, and looked very smug for a moment. 'If I were you, I'd take my advice and keep quiet, Alicia.'

'You're very sure of yourself.'

'Dex adores me…I turn him on in ways you never will.' Maddie smiled. 'He loves the excitement of being around me. You could say I hold all the cards.'

'Not quite,' Alicia said with quiet emphasis, and rested her hand against her stomach. 'I think I have the ace.'

She was rewarded by a brief flash of disquiet in the other woman's eyes. Then she walked away towards the car, her head held high.

Alicia had intended to go straight home. But the thought of the empty house waiting for her made the notion frightening. She felt so low, so confused. Maddie's words kept going around and around in her mind like instruments of torture.

Suddenly she thought of Peter. What was it he had said to her on her wedding day? If you ever need anything…' Well, she had never been more in need of a good friend. She'd go mad if she didn't have someone to talk to, someone who genuinely cared about her.

She glanced at her watch. It was past ten o'clock, but knowing Peter he would still be up.

CHAPTER NINE

'ALLI, what a pleasant surprise!' Peter stood back from the doorway to let her come in. 'Is Dex with you?' He looked out of the door, as if at any moment Dex would come hurrying after her.

'No. I'm all on my own.' Alicia tried to keep her voice light, but it wavered appallingly. 'I'm not disturbing you, am I?' She glanced around the stylish lounge. The house seemed deserted.

'No. I was just finishing off some work in the darkroom.' Peter looked at her closely. 'Everything OK?'

'Not really.' Alicia took a deep breath. She needed a moment or two to gather herself together before telling him what had happened, otherwise it would be very easy to break down and cry. 'Tell you what. You finish up what you were doing and I'll make us a coffee.'

'OK, give me a shout when it's ready.'

Alicia had no problem finding her way around Peter's kitchen. She had spent many hours here in the past, and it felt almost like home.

The house was very modern, a sprawling mansion built on two levels, with a large outside deck overlooking the sea. She carried the tray out to the deck before calling him.

'You don't mind if we sit outside, do you?' she asked as he came up to join her.

'No, I prefer it.' He sat down in the chair opposite. 'You look nice, by the way,' he commented, his eyes drifting over her long red dress.

'I've just escaped from the most awful party.' Alicia

leaned her head back against her chair and looked up at the sky. It was a very bright night, the sky sparkled like a dark piece of crushed velvet studded with diamanté.

'So what's the matter?' he asked gently.

'Dex is having an affair. Well, I suppose if I'm going to be truthful I have to say that he's never really loved me at all.' She closed her eyes; it seemed easier to tell him the whole story that way. She felt such a fool.

After she had finished there was a long silence. She looked at him then, her heart beating slowly, unevenly against her chest. 'I'm an idiot, aren't I?'

'No…oh, Alicia, of course not.' He sat forward earnestly.

'What should I do, Peter?' Her voice was an urgent plea, her eyes wide and shimmering with unshed tears now.

'You must leave him.'

The quiet words shocked her. 'I can't.'

'Why on earth not?'

She reached to pick up her coffee. 'Peter, I'm pregnant. I rely on him for my job, for my home…I've nowhere to go.' Hidden behind all that were the unspoken words that she still loved him. She didn't want to leave him. She hated herself for being so weak.

'Maddie threatened that if I gave Dex an ultimatum she'd pull the plug on their business dealings…it could bankrupt him.'

'Do you give a damn?'

Alicia gave a shake of her head. 'Not for myself.'

'Hell, Alicia, I can't believe that you still care about him so much…after what he's done!'

'He doesn't deserve to lose everything,' Alicia said quietly.

'She could be bluffing, to try and keep you silent so you don't spoil their affair.'

'Maybe, but I'm not so sure. I think she could be vindictive enough.'

'And maybe they both just deserve each other. To be honest, I've had suspicions about Dex and Maddie for a while now.' Peter took a deep breath. 'She was over at his apartment the morning of your wedding.'

Alicia felt her heart thundering against her breast. 'How do you know that?'

'I saw her there.' He grimaced. 'I called over to take a few photos of Dex with his best man. She was there and...'

'And?' Alicia looked at him sharply.

'Her lipstick was all mussed up. They'd obviously been kissing.'

Alicia moved suddenly and her cup spilt over, down on to her dress, soaking the red material with an ugly brown stain. She waved Peter away as he sprang up to help her. 'Why didn't you tell me?' she gasped.

'How could I tell you, Alli?' His voice was miserable. 'It was the day of your wedding. I was torn in two.'

Alicia bit down on her lip and her eyes filled with tears. 'I've been such a damn fool,' she murmured, and through her tears she felt anger...an anger of such force and intensity that it took her breath away.

'What should I do?' She looked over at Peter.

'I've told you. Leave him,' Peter said firmly. 'You can come and live here with me. I've plenty of room for you and Vicky.'

Alicia stared at him in astonishment. 'I can't do that.'

'Why not?'

'Because...' She shook her head. 'It would make everything a hell of a lot worse. Dex would think I was having an affair with you.'

'Do you care what he thinks?'

'I...' Alicia shook her head helplessly. Why should she

care? But, strangely, she did. 'It would just make everything worse,' she reiterated weakly.

'OK.' Peter nodded calmly. 'Then how's this for an idea?
You can take my apartment in Sydney. It's large, with three
bedrooms. I only go there once in a while on business; the
rest of the time it stands empty.'

'I couldn't, Peter.' She shook her head and got up to find
a cloth to try and clean her dress.

'I don't see why not.' He followed her into the house.

'For one thing, how would I live?' She went through to
the kitchen and tore some kitchen roll to absorb the spilt
coffee.

'Easy. I've loads of contacts. You could get yourself a
good office job.'

'In my condition?'

'Why not?' He shrugged. 'You've a better chance of
getting work in a big city. Anyway, money needn't be a
problem. I'm a very wealthy man.'

She frowned, wishing that she could think straight. 'I
couldn't put on you like that. Besides, I've got Vicky to
think about.'

'Vicky is seventeen,' Peter pointed out. 'And anyway,
she's broken up from school now. There's no better time
for a move.' He watched as she rubbed ineffectually at the
stain on her dress.

For a long while she didn't speak, didn't look up. 'He
really wants this baby,' she said at last. 'It doesn't seem
right to take it away from him.'

'He should have thought about that before he started
playing around, then, shouldn't he?' Peter said calmly.

Peter's words played over and over in her mind as she
drove home along the coast. He was right.

She wanted this baby so much...wanted it to have a father, wanted to play happy families. But she was living a lie and so was Dex. He wanted his baby, but he also wanted Maddie.

The only thing to do, to save her self-respect, was leave. Even as she said the words to herself she felt bereft at the idea.

The narrow winding road was deserted. The moon lit it up like a silver ribbon against the dark green backdrop of the rainforest.

She wondered if Dex would be home yet, or if he had given up all ghost of pretence and stayed with Maddie?

Anger assailed her again at that thought. What was it Maddie had said to him tonight? 'Nobody can have everything.'

She turned the car off the road and down the lane towards her house. It was completely in darkness. Obviously Dex had decided he *could* have everything and had decided to stay at the party.

She parked the car and went inside. The cool of the air-conditioning was a relief after the intense heat of the night. She poured herself a glass of water from the fridge and then went through to the bedroom.

'Where the hell have you been until now?' Dex's voice met her as she walked through the door.

Shocked, she stared at him. He was sitting on the side of the bed, still fully dressed.

'I…I thought you were still at Maddie's,' she said, frowning.

'I've been home a while and I was starting to get worried.'

'Oh, save me the phoney concern, Dex,' she muttered with resentment. She kicked off her shoes and put her drink on her bedside table.

'Where have you been?' he asked again.

'If you must know I called in to see Peter.' She sat down on the bed, her back to him, and reached to unfasten her zipper.

'Good old Pete was able to alleviate all those symptoms of tiredness and boredom, was he?' Dex's voice dripped with sarcasm, making her temper rise.

How dared he poke fun at her? 'As a matter of fact he did.' She slanted him a very cold look. 'And don't pretend that you give a damn, because you and I both know we haven't got that kind of marriage.'

A silence followed her words; a silence loaded with tension.

'Really? So what kind of marriage *have* we got?' Dex's calmness infuriated her.

'I suppose you'd call it a marriage of convenience…a marriage made on a piece of paper for the sake of a child.' Her voice was rising rapidly. She wanted to hit out, hurt him, make him feel as wounded and as small as she felt. 'A marriage without love…'

'I didn't realise you were so unhappy,' he said calmly.

She glanced over at him. He was regarding her steadily, a shuttered expression on the handsome face. She felt her anger subside as quickly as it had risen, leaving only a pain inside, a pain that was so deep it felt as if it would never be assuaged.

She reached again to unfasten her zip. It had snagged on a piece of material and wouldn't come free.

Calmly Dex reached across and helped her, sliding the zip down easily. The touch of his hands against her skin made her temperature rise. She still wanted him, she realised with a feeling of helplessness. Still longed for his love, for his closeness.

She flinched away from him and his hand dropped to his side.

She picked up her nightdress and went to get undressed in the bathroom, closing the door with a quiet finality. She couldn't allow herself to weaken when Dex touched her. He had been holding another woman in his arms tonight, for heaven's sake!

When she returned to the bedroom Dex was in bed and the light had been turned off. She slipped between the sheets and lay stiffly apart from him, staring up into the darkness.

Neither spoke. The silence resounded in Alicia's ears. She wondered what he was thinking, or maybe he was asleep. She closed her eyes and tried to relax, tried not to think about how good it would be to lie in his arms. She had to be strong.

It was the early hours of the morning before Alicia finally drifted to sleep. It seemed just a few moments later when the shrill ring of the phone woke her.

Feeling groggy, she glanced at the bedside clock. It was ten o'clock; they had overslept! Then she remembered it was Saturday and relaxed. She reached out and answered the phone. 'Hello? Oh, hi, Peter.' She pushed a strand of hair out of her eyes and sat up slightly.

Next to her, Dex stirred. She glanced down at the broad contours of his naked back and felt the tension that had kept her from sleeping last night return. Dex was having an affair. It wasn't some bad dream; it was happening.

'Hi. Haven't woken you, have I?' Peter asked brightly.

'It's OK,' Alicia murmured.

'It's just that I've got an idea for you. I've rung around a few contacts in Sydney this morning and I've got you a job...it's only for a month or two at most, but I think you should seriously consider it.'

'A job? Doing what?'

'Hold on to your hat.' Peter sounded smug. 'Modelling maternity wear.'

'Modelling!' Alicia felt dazed by the suggestion.

'Yeah…look, don't laugh. It's big business. And I've got a top designer who's really interested in you. Plus there's all the spin-offs, features in magazines…'

'Oh, Peter, how many favours have you pulled in to get this for me?' she asked incredulously.

'They're keen. They've already seen your portfolio that I sent. We could be talking big money…plus it's a short-term contract—two months or so. I think it would be ideal for you. You can stay at my apartment in Sydney, and it will give you freedom and space to think about what you want to do.'

Alicia didn't say anything for a while. Her mind was racing. She didn't want to leave Dex, but she couldn't go on like this. Peter did have a point. A couple of months apart might be sensible…might give them both a chance to think about what they wanted. Then again it might be playing straight into Maddie's hands, a small voice cautioned.

She glanced helplessly over at Dex. He was awake, lying on his back now, staring up at the ceiling as she spoke.

'Can I have some time to think about this?' she asked Peter.

'Don't take too long. They are keen, but then again there is a hell of a lot of competition out there.'

'I understand.' Alicia's voice wavered for a second. 'And Peter…thanks for thinking about me.'

The silence in the bedroom was almost overwhelming after she put the phone down.

'What was all that about?' Dex grated.

'Peter's found me a job…modelling maternity wear…' Her voice faltered, and she just looked at him helplessly.

'Incredible.' Dex's voice was dry. 'I suppose that's why you went to see him last night.'

'No, I—'

'Went pouring out your heart? Told him all about our loveless marriage, and how trapped it makes you feel?' The sarcasm in his voice grated over her raw nerves. 'And good old Pete has immediately put it right for you, gone out, pulled in favours and got you a modelling job. Helps to know the right people, doesn't it?'

Alicia didn't argue about that; she knew that never in a million years would she have been offered a modelling job if it wasn't for Peter.

'I suppose it's in Sydney?'

She nodded. 'He's offered me his apartment there.'

Dex's features darkened. 'Very cosy. What's he getting in return?'

'What do you mean?'

'Do I have to spell it out? What's Peter's piece of the action? Are you going to pay him rent in kind?'

Anger flooded through Alicia, making her skin burn bright red. 'How dare you say something so disgusting? Peter is a decent, honourable man. He would never take advantage of me.'

Dex's expression was scathing. 'Anyway, I won't allow you to go.' He sat up in bed. The morning sun glinted on the broad, powerful chest; the sheets were low on the hard, flat abdomen. Somehow his vital attractiveness added to her fury. She wanted him, and that fact ate at her with disgust. He was a liar and a cheat.

'Don't you tell me what I can and cannot do,' she warned him quietly. 'I'm going.'

Suddenly Dex's anger dropped like a mask. 'I don't want you to go, Alli. You're my wife, damn it. You have a child to consider.'

'I'm considering my child,' she grated furiously. 'I'm just trying to think what is best for us all. You, me and the baby.'

'I thought we had already decided on what was best.' He reached to touch her but she pulled away. 'You agreed with me that we should be a family, that we could make it work.'

'But it's not working out, is it, Dex?' Her heart thumped wildly against her breast.

'And you think running away is going to make it better?' His voice became gentle. 'Let's talk about this, Alli. I know you've been feeling bored recently. I've been neglecting you.'

'You can say that again,' she snapped. It was on the tip of her tongue to hurl Maddie at him, but he spoke first.

'It's pressure of work, but it will get better.'

She pushed back the covers of the bed and got up. 'You're a liar, Dexter. Things aren't going to get any better. At least be truthful with yourself if you can't be truthful to me. We don't love each other.'

For a moment he said nothing, just looked at her. Her eyes seemed impossibly large for her small face; they seemed to look right into the depths of his soul, to tear at him.

'Give me one good reason to stay,' she asked him suddenly, her voice the merest whisper.

'You're going to have my baby—'

He broke off as she turned away from him.

'We have an agreement, Alli—'

'I'm not in the mood to talk about our agreement.' She released her hair from the grips that had held it up during the night. It tumbled luxuriously around her shoulders. She crossed to the wardrobes and took out a dress to wear.

She had never felt more conscious of Dex's scrutiny. She

felt his eyes moving over the soft curves of her body as she moved, almost as if they were his hands.

'So what *are* you in the mood for?' he asked suddenly, as she came back to stand beside the bed to pick up her hairbrush. The harsh rasp of his voice was filled with a taunting sensuality.

She glanced down at him, her eyes wide.

'Are you in the mood for sex? Now *there's* something we do well together...remember?'

She flinched at the cool sarcasm. 'I'm not going to talk to you while you're in this mood,' she whispered unsteadily.

'That's OK. I don't want to talk anyway.' He reached up and caught her arm, pulling her down towards the bed.

'Dex, stop it.' She tried to twist away from him, the brush dropping from her hand. He pinned her by her wrists to the soft satin covers of the bed.

'Stop it!' She tried to twist her head away, but his lips came down against hers in a hard, punishing kiss.

Despite everything she found herself kissing him back. He released her hands and found the front fastener of her nightdress.

Her breathing was fast and heavy. She hated herself for wanting him so much, kept reminding herself that yesterday he had been holding another woman in his arms. But all those thoughts seemed to be swept away in the greater tide of passion as he kissed her again.

'That's better.' Dex's lips curved in a taunting line. 'You belong to me, Alicia. We have an agreement, whether you want to talk about it or not.'

He pulled her nightdress off. His skin was against hers. The feel of him, the taste of him against her lips, made her stop fighting. She started to kiss him back, meeting his fiery demands with equal intensity, her anger lending her passion a bittersweet edge.

Dex's lovemaking was unlike anything she had ever experienced with him before. His passion was assertive, commanding, possessive. It turned her on so much that she hated herself. But she couldn't tell him to stop. It was exciting, sensual…it lifted her to exhilarating heights of arousal.

As she peaked she cried out his name, ecstasy and despair mingling in her voice.

He rolled away, his breathing uneven in the silence.

Her heart was racing; her body burned from his touch. She cringed as she thought about how she had responded to him. Had she no pride?

'Well, you've proved one thing.' Her voice trembled. She didn't dare look at him. 'You're stronger than I am.'

'Oh, come on, Alli.' He rolled over and looked down at her. 'I pulled back before going too far. You could have told me to stop. You could have pushed me away. You responded, you went along—'

'Yes…maybe.' She couldn't in all honesty argue with that. She reached for her nightgown, pulling it over her naked body with shaking hands.

'I didn't hurt you…did I?'

She looked at him then. She noticed a muscle pulsing at the edge of his cheek.

'Not physically, no.' She felt the need to be truthful, then promptly regretted it when she saw the look of regret in the darkness of his eyes.

'Alicia…the last thing I want is to hurt you in any way. But—'

'But if we stay together that's what we're going to continue doing to each other.' Her voice was filled with despair. The knowledge that Dex didn't love her, that his lovemaking had been merely proving a point to her, showing her what they shared together in a fierce reminder of his claim over her body, was almost more than she could bear.

Dex didn't reply.

She got up from the bed and went through to the bathroom.

She showered and dressed, feeling strangely numb. No matter how much she tried to work out what she should do, her mind refused to function.

She made herself look presentable, and then wandered down the hallway in search of her husband.

The smell of freshly ground coffee greeted her as she walked into the kitchen. Dex had the back door open and was standing out on the porch, a cup in his hand. He was dressed in beige shorts and a lightweight shirt. He looked casual, relaxed and incredibly attractive.

He turned as he heard her coming in. His eyes flicked over her appearance. In those few seconds he seemed to miss nothing; the fact that she wore make-up to cover the pallor of her skin, the shadows in her eyes…he took everything in at a glance.

'Do you feel OK?' His voice was tense.

'Yes, thank you,' she lied. They sounded like two polite strangers. After their lovemaking, the incongruity was almost absurd.

'There's coffee in the pot,' he said, turning back to his contemplation of the morning.

'Thanks.' She poured herself a cup and then glanced over at him.

The back of the house looked out towards the rainforest. Densely green, it tumbled down the mountainside towards the sea. They could have been completely alone in the world. It was wild, unspoilt and spectacularly beautiful.

She would have given anything to go and snuggle in next to him, lean her head against his broad chest and tell him she loved him. Her pride rebelled furiously at the notion, yet the need for him continued to eat away at her.

'I've been thinking,' he said slowly. 'You're right. Maybe you should take this job in Sydney.'

Alicia stared at the broad contours of his back. Now that he had agreed with her, perversely she felt nothing but pain and disappointment.

'We don't want to make each other unhappy,' he continued.

Silence lay between them, filled with nothing but the sounds of the forest outside. Two white cockatoos were having a squabble over a branch of a tree at the bottom of the garden, the noise loud and startling.

The heat of the day was intense, the sky an electric blue, it felt almost like an airtight lid on the perfect day.

He looked back at her then, waiting for her to say something.

'It's a possible two-month contract.' She forced herself to be rational, yet she found herself wanting to backtrack. Wanting to tell him she would stay.

'I probably won't be able to work much longer than that. Indeed, I might not even be offered a job at all; it's not definite.'

'But Peter's apartment is waiting and the opportunity beckons.' His voice was dry.

'We'll treat it as a trial separation, shall we?' she said breathlessly.

He raked a hand through his hair and shook his head. 'Whatever.' There was pain in the darkness of his eyes.

'I'll ring you every day, and you think about what you want.' Her voice was very unsteady now.

He returned to his contemplation of the morning.

'Fine. Go to Sydney, Alicia. Chase the dream.'

He took a deep breath. Letting her go had to be the hardest thing he had ever done. But she wanted her career, and he could either give in gracefully or end up with her hating him.

CHAPTER TEN

'MOVE your head a little to the left, Alicia.'

She did as she was asked. The bright arc lights were hot, and she felt uncomfortable.

'A little more, please,' the photographer asked again. 'That's it, hold it...that's wonderful.'

How long would she have to sit like this? she wondered. It was the most awkward, stupid position.

She was sitting in a very modern studio. There was a whole team of people watching her: the make-up artist, the hairdresser, Pat Malony from IMAGES modelling agency, two photographers, plus another few shadowy people who stood in the background, discussing the whole thing.

She had been modelling for over a month now, and it didn't seem to be getting easier. It was unbelievably hard work. Today they had been inside the studio from very early, she hadn't seen daylight for hours, just these blinding lights. In the previous weeks they'd had her out in all sorts of weird and wonderful clothing, irrespective of the weather.

The only thing that could be said about it all was that she had made some new friends...some of the other models, and Pat from the agency. Without them life in Sydney would have been intolerable. Then there was the money. She could hardly believe the amount she was earning, and it seemed to be going up and up with each new offer of work that came in.

'Give me one of those wistful smiles,' the photographer asked now.

How long would they make her sit like this?

She thought about Dex. It was his birthday today. He would be twenty-eight. She missed him; she wouldn't have believed how much she could miss him. At night she lay alone in bed and her body ached for him. By day her thoughts were more frequently in Queensland than they were here. Then there was Vicky; she missed her too.

Vicky had flown up to Sydney with her, but she had only stayed two weeks, helping her to settle in, taking in the sights, then she had become bored. She'd missed her friends, and most of all she'd missed her new boyfriend, Robbie. No amount of persuasion had induced her to stay.

Dex had given her a summer job in his office. He said she was quite good, that she knew her way around computers and was handling things in a responsible and mature manner.

She spoke on the phone to both of them every day. Mostly she called in the evening, but today she had rung early, to wish Dex a happy birthday, to ask if he liked the cuff-links she had bought for him.

She wondered what he had thought about his birthday card. She had spent hours choosing it; she must have read every verse in every card in the shop. She hadn't wanted to send anything too slushy, too sentimental; her pride wouldn't allow that. And anyway, Dex would probably think she had gone mad. Then again she hadn't wanted to send something that was too cool. She had needed to hit a happy medium.

She hadn't been able to find anything and in the end had just given up and bought one that said 'Happy Birthday to My Husband'. Then, annoyed with herself, she had signed it; 'love always, Alicia'.

Now she was worried about the words. Her lips curved

in a sad smile. Imagine weighing words to this extent, even on a card! She was going crazy.

'Perfect.' The photographer shouted, his tone ecstatic. 'That is going to be wonderful.'

'Great, can I move now?'

'Yeah…you can take a break.'

Pat came across to her. She was a smart woman in her early thirties, with short dark hair and a friendly, genuine smile. 'That was fabulous, Alli. You're a natural.'

'Literally.' Alicia grinned and patted her stomach. She was five and a half months pregnant, and although she was carrying the pregnancy neatly there was no doubting now that she was definitely with child.

'We're going to call it a day, ladies.' The photographer came up behind them. 'I think we've got all we want.'

Alicia sighed in relief. She'd had enough.

'Fancy a coffee?' Pat asked her. 'A few of the girls are going down to The Rocks for a drink.'

Alicia nodded. 'I'd enjoy the company, thanks.'

A little while later they emerged in a group outside the building. The city street was vibrating with traffic, with people. There was a hint of rain in the air, a damp coolness which brought a chill to Alicia's bones after the heat of Queensland.

The girls were talking about a fashion shoot they were all to do tomorrow.

'Hey, Alicia, look.' One of them took her arm and led her towards a news-stand. 'It's you.' She pointed to the cover of a magazine.

Alicia's picture stared back at her. It had been taken a few weeks ago; she was sitting with a toddler next to her and a handsome dark-haired man leaning over her shoulder. Underneath, it said, 'How to get through pregnancy and still look sexy, and ten super summer knits for your new baby.'

Alicia smiled. 'It doesn't look like me,' she said, wondering how they had made her seem so glamorous.

'I wouldn't mind playing husband and wife with him…playing anything, in fact,' one of the girls said, stabbing a finger at the picture of the male model.

All the girls laughed, and they turned into the coffee bar which was a favourite haunt for people from the agency. They found a table in the window and placed their orders with a waiter.

'Pat was saying that you've separated from your husband,' Tara, one of the models, remarked. 'So have I. Divorce is the next step, I suppose.' She continued blithely on, not noticing the colour draining away from Alicia's skin.

Their drinks arrived. Pat changed the subject. But Alicia couldn't concentrate on anything else that was said.

She didn't want a divorce.

She felt a sick lurch inside at the thought that perhaps Dex wouldn't really want her back…that she had made a mistake leaving. She had hoped this time apart would help, that it would give him a chance to think about what he wanted, a chance to maybe miss her. But in fact every time she spoke to him on the phone he sounded more and more distant.

This morning he had hardly had time to speak to her at all, and she had asked Vicky if everything was all right.

'Oh, he's been in a mood all week,' she had muttered sagely. 'He's working too hard, that's all. Pay no attention.'

Well, to hell with him anyway, she thought angrily now. If he didn't want her she could do without him. In fact she was managing fine.

She remembered how he had driven her and Vicky to

the airport in Cairns, had carried their luggage inside for them.

'So, you've got everything you need?' he had said as they'd queued at the counter to check in.

She had met his eyes over Vicky's head. She had wanted to say no—*No, I need you.*

But she hadn't, of course, and she wouldn't. She wouldn't go back unless he begged her on his hands and knees, and even then she'd have to think about it. The tough thought cheered her.

She was doing really well on her own. Her bank account was healthy, and one of the photographers had even asked her out on a date last week. She had turned him down, of course, but it had built her confidence. If Dex didn't want her that was fine; there were plenty of other men in the water. She would just get herself a fishing licence.

Her confident, fighting mood waned a little as she remembered saying goodbye to Dex.

He hadn't even had the time to wait around to see them off; he had helped with the luggage and then been in a hurry to get back to town. Work...or Maddie...had come first. Every time she felt herself weakening, missing him, she thought about that.

Vicky had kissed him on the cheek. 'I probably won't be staying away long,' she had told him. 'Robbie is trying to get tickets for a rock concert next month, and I said I'd like to go with him.'

Dex had smiled affectionately at his sister-in-law. 'Have a good time. And just give me a ring when you want to come home. I'll pick you up from the airport.'

But when Dex had looked at her his eyes had been cool, no hint of any emotion whatsoever. Maybe he simply hadn't cared.

'Goodbye, then, Dex.' She had been equally cool. She could hide her emotions with the best.

He had nodded, and had taken her into his arms. The familiar scent of his cologne, the comfort of his arms, the warm, gentle sensation of tenderness had been fleeting.

'You take care,' he had whispered against her ear. 'And take care of junior, you hear?'

Then he had walked away from her without a backward glance. Her last view of him had been distorted with tears. A tall, handsome man disappearing amidst the crowds.

'So what do you think?' Pat's voice brought her back to the present with a start.

'Sorry?' She glanced across at her with wide, apologetic eyes and the woman laughed.

'You haven't heard a word we've been saying, have you?'

Alicia shook her head. 'I was miles away.'

'We were admiring this guy.' Pat nodded her head out towards the street.

'I do hope he's going to come in here,' Tara purred.

Alicia glanced out through the window. There was a man locking a very snazzy red sports car. He had his back to her. He was tall and dark, and he was wearing an expensive-looking suit, probably some kind of designer label. Something about his build and the way he moved reminded her of Dex.

She looked sharply away. Everything reminded her of Dex, she thought, feeling annoyed with herself. 'It's very hot and stuffy in here. Would anyone like a glass of water?' she asked, looking around to catch a waiter's attention, but there was none about.

No one at the table answered her, their eyes were all riveted looking out of the window.

With a sigh, Alicia stood up and walked towards the bar,

deciding it would probably be faster in the long run to order her drink there.

The place was very busy. The long, polished wooden counter was lined with bar stools, most of them taken by people sipping cappuccinos and exotic types of coffee. The smell of roasting coffee beans and sweet Danish pastries filled the air. After a few moments the couple sitting nearest to her left, and she sat down on one of the vacated stools.

'Can I buy you a drink?' The familiar voice from a few stools down made her turn. It was the photographer who had asked her out last week.

'Oh, Andy. I didn't see you there.' She smiled at him. 'No, thanks, I'm just getting myself a glass of water. I'm really hot. The girls are sitting in the window,' she told him, in a friendly attempt to get rid of him.

'OK, but don't forget we've got a date tomorrow morning. Nine o'clock sharp.'

'Oh, I won't forget,' she assured him with a grin.

'Am I interrupting something?'

The deep voice close to her ear made a shiver of astonishment prickle down the fine hairs at the back of her neck.

She swivelled around on her seat and her eyes met with Dex's. She couldn't say anything; she just stared at him in wonder. For a second she thought maybe she was asleep and dreaming. He was the man from outside, the man in the dark stylish suit.

'It's you!' she said finally.

He grinned, and it was that attractive, wonderful grin that made her blood race. 'I hope so.'

'What are you doing here?'

'Looking for you. I called the agency and they sent me over to the studio, then the studio told me I might find you here.'

The assistant behind the bar came to serve them. 'A flat white coffee,' Dex requested, and then looked at Alicia.

'Just a mineral water for me, thanks.'

Dex drew up the bar stool next to her. Then he glanced down towards Andy, who was in the process of leaving.

'I'm so surprised to see you,' Alicia said, in what had to be the understatement of the year.

'I wanted to surprise you.' He returned his attention to her, and his eyes slipped over her appearance with open admiration. 'I almost didn't recognise you when I came in.'

She was wearing a cream trouser suit and a round-neck navy silk top. She tried not to blush. 'I've put on a few pounds.'

'You look fabulous,' he said, his dark eyes gentle and sincere. 'Very…' He paused, searching for the right word.

'Earth mother?' she supplied with a rueful grin.

'Sophisticated,' he said firmly. 'I like your hair.'

'Thank you.' She smiled shyly. She had had it styled at a top salon last week. Although they had kept the length it had been layered, giving it structure and shape.

'I'm glad you didn't get it cut short.'

'Are you?' Her heart was bouncing crazily against her chest.

'Yes.' He reached across and stroked a golden lock of it back from her face. 'I've always thought that you have incredibly sexy hair.'

She laughed breathlessly at the absurdity of that remark. 'How can anyone have sexy hair?'

'I don't know…' He frowned. 'But you have.'

Their drinks arrived; they didn't touch them. Just continued to sit there, staring at each other.

Any minute now I'm going to wake up, Alicia thought with a tinge of panic.

His gaze moved from her face to her hand, which was

resting against the counter. Her engagement and wedding rings sparkled brilliantly under the halogen lights of the bar.

'Who was the guy that was talking to you?'

'Just a photographer. We're doing a fashion shoot together tomorrow,' she said, her manner dismissive. 'What on earth are you doing here, Dex?' she asked him quietly. 'I mean why didn't you tell me you were coming when we spoke on the phone this morning.'

'For one thing I didn't have time to tell you. I'd a million and one things to do before catching my plane.' He smiled wryly. 'And, as I said, I wanted to surprise you. It was a spur-of-the-moment decision last night, to come and see what you're up to.'

'Not much, as you can see.' She smiled.

'You're not doing too badly for yourself.' He slanted her a droll look. 'I keep seeing you in magazines, striking various poses with an array of exotic-looking males.'

Her heart missed a beat, and then pumped furiously hard. Was he jealous? Please let him be jealous, she prayed, then felt like a ridiculous child. 'It's not as glamorous as it looks,' she told him truthfully.

'Well I thought I'd come and see for myself what kind of life you're leading these days.' He leaned closer. 'Check up that you're looking after junior.'

Reality slanted through the misty haze of her dream-like trance. That was why he was here. 'Of course I am.' Her voice hardened.

'I can see that. You look so radiant.' He smiled. 'How have you been?'

'Never better,' she assured him brightly. 'What about you?'

'Apart from being another year older...OK.' He shrugged.

'As long as you're not deeper in debt.' She smiled.

'Oh, thanks,' he said wryly.

She had to laugh.

'I'm all cheered up now,' he said sardonically.

'Happy birthday.' She leaned forward and touched her lips against his cheek in a brief contact. At one time if she had done that she would have kissed him on the lips as well, or he would have reached out and kissed her back.

She felt awkward and embarrassed as she pulled away from him. She couldn't look him in the eye. It was really hard trying to be cool and dispassionate with a man you felt so deeply about.

He didn't love her and he didn't want her, she reminded herself fiercely. All he was interested in was his child. That was why he was here.

Someone jogged his elbow. 'Shall we get out of here?' he asked suddenly. 'It really is getting very crowded.'

She nodded, and watched as he left some money on the counter for their drinks. Then together they made their way outside.

'Where did you get this car?' she asked, mesmerised as he unlocked the shiny red sports car.

'Rented it at the airport.'

'I see you chose the family model,' she jibed with a grin.

'I thought I'd go for the babe magnet while I still could,' he joked, starting up the engine with a powerful roar.

'Before the baby chair in the back spoils the image?' She laughed.

'Something like that. What do you think? Are you magnetised?'

'Not by the car.' The words just slipped out before she could check them.

'Does that mean I might get more than a peck on the cheek for my birthday kiss?' he asked with a raised eyebrow.

'Dex, I—'

Whatever she had started to say was cut short when he leaned across and kissed her on the lips.

It was a fleeting caress, firm, dominant, deliciously sensual.

Then he moved back. 'That's better,' he said decisively.

She couldn't find breath to say anything. Her heart was pumping unevenly against her chest. But there was no love in that kiss, she reminded herself sharply.

'I thought we'd go and have dinner together. What do you think?' he asked her now.

She nodded. 'Good idea.'

Over his shoulder her eyes focused on the coffee shop. In the window, sitting watching her with expressions of complete astonishment, were the girls from the modelling agency.

'Oh, no!' Alicia's cheeks flooded with embarrassed colour.

'What is it?' Dex looked at her in alarm.

'I was with some friends inside. I forgot all about them. I didn't even tell them I was going.'

'Is that all?' He shook his head. 'Do you want to go back inside and tell them you're leaving with me?'

'I think they already know.' Alicia nodded towards the window. 'They're watching us.'

Dex looked around. 'That's all right, then.' He gave the girls a wave and a smile, then smoothly pulled out into the flow of traffic. 'You can explain to them tomorrow.'

The startled expressions on her friends' faces made Alicia start to giggle.

'What's so funny?' Dex looked at her in puzzlement.

'Oh, nothing.' Alicia remembered how Tara's mouth had been hanging open and giggled again. 'It's just that I don't think they realise that you're my husband…in fact I know they don't.'

'You mean they think you're a flirtatious flibbertigibbet?' Dex asked teasingly.

'Probably…and in my condition too.'

'You've never looked more beautiful,' Dex said softly.

The note in his voice stilled her amusement. 'Dex, don't try to sweet-talk me,' she warned in a low tone.

'I wasn't trying to sweet-talk you.' His voice darkened.

'Good.' She stared out at the streets, keeping her head turned well away from him. Because it just wouldn't work, she told herself fiercely. Dex had given up all rights to her when he had taken Maddie McDowell to bed. She wasn't going to allow him to just pick up with her when the mood struck him. She had far too much pride and self-esteem for that.

CHAPTER ELEVEN

THEY found a place to park the car and walked to the Harbour.

The sun was going down and the sky was a flamingo-pink; it looked washed and fresh after the rain of the day. The breeze that blew in from the sea was warm and gentle.

They stood and watched as one of the ferries pulled out from port. It rounded the corner to sail past the Opera House and down towards Manly.

'It's a lovely city, isn't it?' Alicia said as they walked on towards the waterside restaurants. 'A bit on the cold side sometimes.'

Dex laughed at that. 'It's hardly cold! You've just got used to the tropics of Queensland. Now if you'd ever experienced a winter in Boston…*that's cold*.'

'Do you ever miss your home?'

'I don't miss the winters.' Dex smiled. 'But Boston is a beautiful city. Speaking of which, my mother phoned the other day and she was asking after you. She's delighted about her first grandchild.'

'Is she?' Alicia's tone was flat.

'Mmm. She was a bit concerned when she heard you were in Sydney on your own.'

'Well, tell her not to worry one little bit. That I'm fine,' Alicia said brightly, 'and I love Sydney.'

'I'm sure that will put her mind at rest,' Dex said, a dry note creeping into his tone.

Alicia bit down on her lip. She'd liked Dex's mother; she hated to think that she might be upsetting her or worrying her. 'If you give me her phone number I'll ring and speak to her myself.'

Dex didn't say anything to that.

A busker was playing a saxophone on the walkway, and the haunting melody drifted with them on the breeze. People were walking down towards the Opera House, some of them dressed in long evening gowns, some in casual clothing.

They reached the restaurant, and a waiter led them across the terrace to a table at the water's edge.

'You'll like the food here,' Alicia said as they reached for the menus that had been left for them on the table. 'It's really very good.'

The lights from the skyscrapers started to brighten up the darkening sky and the Opera House was illuminated in a brilliant wash of blue colour.

'It's not usually that colour,' Alicia told Dex as he commented on how lovely it looked. 'They've lit it in blue for a festival that's on at the moment. It's a fabulous building. I went to a show there last week and it was excellent.'

'You seem to be getting out a lot. Dinner, the theatre. It's certainly an exciting life in the city.'

'I'm enjoying it.' Alicia forced herself to sound positive. She wouldn't allow him to know just how lonely she had been without him.

She glanced over at him and studied him surreptitiously as he looked through the menu.

The candlelight was flickering over the contours of his face, highlighting the high cheekbones, the almost autocratic, powerful good looks. His hair gleamed jet-black, and his suit sat with finesse upon the width of his shoulders. She noticed the gleam of the gold cuff-links that she had bought him for his birthday. She wondered if he had got her card...

He glanced up and caught her watching him.

'Where's Vicky tonight?' she asked, trying to cover her awkwardness.

'She's staying over at her friend Jenny's house.'

'I take it when I spoke to her on the phone this morning she already knew you were coming here today?'

'Yes. She thought it was a good idea for me to surprise you.' He grinned. 'She's a good kid.'

'How's she doing around the office?'

'Not bad. But then, there's not that much to do these days. She's a whizz on the computers.'

'She said she was enjoying the work.' Alicia put her menu down for a moment. 'She's not in the way, is she, Dex?' she asked suddenly. 'I mean, I was in two minds whether or not to allow her to leave Sydney, but she was so insistent. Downright miserable, in fact, when I told her I wanted her to stay here with me—'

'Of course she's not in the way…in the way of what?' Dex frowned, and seemed to be genuinely perplexed by the question. 'That house is her home, Alli. She loves it there.'

'Even so, you've been very kind—offering her that holiday job and putting up with her.'

'I haven't been kind at all.' He shook his head. 'I do need someone part-time around the office, and she's very trustworthy. I think it's more a case of Vicky putting up with me at the moment. I've been damned moody lately.'

'Have you?' Alicia stared at him. That was unusual for Dex; he wasn't really a moody kind of guy. 'Why?'

He hesitated, his dark eyes intense on the questioning, almost eager light in her eyes.

She seemed so young, he thought suddenly. Young and enthusiastic and filled with a love of this new exciting life in Sydney. She wouldn't want to hear why he had been feeling so damned miserable. 'Just the usual.'

'Stresses and strains of becoming a tycoon?' she asked lightly.

'Something like that.'

'Still doing business with Maddie, I take it?' It took all her control to keep her voice civil.

'You could say that.'

There was a note of irony in his voice that she didn't miss. It seemed Maddie McDowell was still very much on the scene, and filling his lonely nights, no doubt. The notion made her blaze with anger.

The candlelight flickered as a sudden breeze caught it, nearly extinguishing it. Alicia watched the flame dancing for a moment, struggling to keep its warm, fiery hold. That candle was a little like their relationship, she thought suddenly. One gust of wind, one wrong turning, and it could be stifled forever.

'So how's the business going?' she asked quickly, trying to banish Maddie to the back of her mind. It didn't do to think about her; it had led to too many sleepless nights.

'I didn't come all this way to talk about the business, Alli,' he said seriously.

Her eyebrows lifted. 'So, what did you come to talk about?'

'Us.'

'Sounds ominous.' Her heart was beating double time now. Had he come to tell her about Maddie? Maybe ask for them to divorce once the baby was born?

'Does it?' His eyes were very serious, his mouth set in a grim line. 'I've been doing a lot of thinking since you went away, and—'

The waiter came to take their order and she was left wondering what on earth he had been going to say.

He ordered a steak and Alicia ordered fish, the first thing

she had seen on the menu. Although she wasn't feeling a bit hungry.

When they were alone again Dex lifted his wine glass and studied her over the rim.

'And?' she prompted him impatiently.

'And I miss you,' he breathed huskily.

'You miss me?' Alicia repeated, exhilaration flooding her.

He nodded. 'I hate you being down here on your own, especially in your condition.'

Alicia stared at him, her elation dying. That was all he was worried about. 'You mean I should be barefoot and pregnant in your kitchen?' she murmured angrily.

'No I do not.' His eyes blazed at that. 'I'm not a male chauvinist, Alli, don't try and pin that label on me.'

'So why do you want me to come home?'

'Because it's where you belong.' His voice was very gentle. 'Because I want to look after you.'

'I don't need looking after.' If only he had said he loved her. But that was wishing for the impossible. All he was bothered about was the baby. As Madeline had once said, he thought he could have everything. Well, she wouldn't go back when he snapped his fingers. And it was damned well arrogant of him to expect that she would.

The soft murmur of conversations around them blended into the uncomfortable silence between them.

'Anyway, I've got a lot of work lined up.' She shrugged. 'I may as well be here earning good money as in Queensland being a burden to you.'

'I don't think of you as a burden,' he said grimly.

'Maybe not, but I feel as if I want a little independence.'

He frowned at that. 'So you are happy?'

His question took her aback. She hesitated. She couldn't

honestly say that she was, but her pride wouldn't let her tell him that.

'Stupid question.' His lips twisted wryly.

Their meals arrived. Alicia had never felt less like eating.

Dex changed the subject. 'I saw you on the front cover of a magazine yesterday morning. You looked sensational.'

'Summer knits for babies and how to look sexy in pregnancy?' She had to smile now. 'A little tacky, don't you think?'

He shrugged. 'You must be proud to be on there. It's a great achievement.'

'The competition is fierce,' Alicia admitted. 'And it did give me a bit of a thrill seeing myself on the cover.'

'What are you doing next?'

'I have a fashion shoot for Rupert Williams tomorrow.' She started to relax a little as the conversation moved away from the highly-charged emotive areas. 'He's designing clothes for certain selected stores on the high street now.'

'I'm impressed. He's right up there with the top designers, isn't he?'

'He's very talented,' Alicia agreed. 'I never thought I'd be able to afford a Rupert Williams label in my wardrobe, but I have a few now. Trouble is they're all maternity wear. I won't want to wear any of them after the baby arrives.'

'The way things are going you'll have other designer labels in your wardrobe by then,' Dex said lightly.

'Maybe.' She glanced over and met his eyes. Obviously he thought she had a successful career ahead of her.

'I am proud of you, Alicia,' he said gently. 'But I'm just concerned about you. I care about you.'

'I know.' Her heart thundered unevenly in her breast; she could hear it in her ears. She did know that deep down he cared about her. It just wasn't in the way she wanted him to.

'I'm not a male chauvinist. You're entitled to your career and your own life. But I…' He hesitated, then seemed to struggle for the right words. 'I just don't want you to forget that I'm the father of your child,' he finished finally.

'I'm not about to forget that, Dex,' she told him coolly, and leaned back in her chair. Was that why he had rushed down here to see her? Had he seen that front cover on the magazine, her with another man and a child, and it had set this panic visit in motion?

Well, let him brood, she thought suddenly. Then maybe he'd know how she had felt when she'd found out about Maddie. 'And really you've no need to worry about me,' she said brightly. 'I'm perfectly happy. I've a busy social life and a rewarding career.'

The dark face was impassive, no flicker of emotion. She wasn't sure if it bothered him or not.

The waiter came to clear away their plates and they ordered a coffee each.

'How long are you here for?' she asked him hesitantly.

'I fly out first thing tomorrow morning.'

She wondered if he planned to stay with her, at Peter's apartment? The thought of the sleeping arrangements launched a fresh attack on her pulses, making them race with a mixture of desire and trepidation.

'I booked two return seats.' Dex regarded her steadily across the table.

She frowned. That was so typical of Dex. He was so sure of himself. So damned arrogant. 'As I've just said,' she retorted firmly, 'I can't go back with you now. I have too much work on.'

'I just hoped…' Dex shrugged.

The breeze ruffled the water beside them, sending the flame of the candle dancing again. Alicia shivered.

'Are you cold?' Dex asked with concern.

'Either that or I'm just tired.' She nodded. 'Do you think we could cancel that coffee and just go home?'

'You mean back to Peter's apartment?' Dex corrected her swiftly.

'Yes, that's what I mean,' she answered, looking away from him and reaching to pick up her handbag. But in truth she didn't know what she meant. At this moment her mind didn't seem able to function properly. Contrary to her strong words rejecting Dex's offer there was a stir of disappointment inside…a feeling that she shouldn't have been so quick to turn him down.

Her heart was telling her one thing; her mind was telling her another.

CHAPTER TWELVE

'NICE place Peter's got here,' Dex commented as she made them both a cup of coffee. 'It's no wonder you're feeling settled.'

'It's OK, isn't it?' Her response was perfunctory. She had more things on her mind than Peter's apartment.

'Has he been down to see you at all?'

'No.' Alicia carried the tray through to the living room and put it on the coffee table. 'But it doesn't matter if he does come; there are three bedrooms.'

Dex was standing with his back to her, looking out of the large picture windows down towards the Harbour. It was a fabulous view even at night; the boats lit up, the buildings awash with colour against the silky black of the water and the sky.

He turned then, and surveyed the stylish decor of the room, the pale carpets and white lamps against the vivid Mediterranean blue of the suite.

She poured his coffee and sat back on the settee.

The dark suit made him look tremendously sexy. Seeing him again was such sweet pleasure. She'd have given anything to go into his arms, make love.

But for him it would just be sex, and she didn't know if she could bear the bittersweet sensations of knowing that right now. So what was she going to do about the sleeping arrangements?

He came towards her and picked up his coffee.

The silence between them seemed so heavy it was almost palpable.

She looked up and their eyes collided.

'Where were you thinking of staying tonight?' She forced herself to voice the question and then promptly wished she hadn't as she saw his eyes darkening with a look of derision.

'Where do you want me to stay?'

He had fielded the question wonderfully; now she was stuck with it. 'Well, to be honest, I'm absolutely exhausted. You're welcome to take one of the spare bedrooms.' She stared up at him, her voice and her features schooled into nonchalant composure.

'If that's what you want,' he answered with equanimity, his eyes raking over the proud way she held her head as she looked up at him.

It wasn't what she wanted at all. She leaned her head back against the softness of the settee and rubbed at her neck. It had started to ache. In fact she felt as if she was aching all over.

'You won't come home with me. You want to sleep in separate rooms. Forgive me if I'm being slow on the up-take, but are you trying to tell me our "marriage of convenience" as you like to put it, is at an end?' he drawled sardonically.

'I'm not trying to tell you anything,' she prevaricated. 'I'm tired, Dex. My back is sore. I was up at seven this morning.'

Still he just stared at her, with that formidable, grim expression on his handsome features. 'I don't think you should be putting in long hours.'

'Dex, I'm not ill. I'm having all my check-ups and—'

'OK, I'm not going to fuss.' He cut across her sharply. 'And for what it's worth I didn't come down here expecting you to sleep with me. I'd kind of got the message when you took yourself off. I did hope, however, that a few weeks apart might make you think about what you're giving up.'

'Giving up?' She shook her head.

'Oh, come on, Alli!' His voice was gruff with impatience. 'You need me. You're having our child and that child needs me. You can play around here all you like, pretending you can have everything, but I don't think you can.'

'That's rich, coming from you.' Her heart was thundering now, with anger, with resentment, with the knowledge that as much as she hated it he was right, she *did* need him, but not for the reasons he was espousing.

'What do you mean by that?'

'You know what I mean. *You* are the one who wants everything.' She rubbed at her neck. She felt so tense, so tightly coiled that she was afraid that one wrong word and she would unravel, make a complete fool of herself. 'And I never said I intended to stay up here.'

'So what do you intend?' He put down his empty coffee cup.

'To fulfil my obligations in the work I took on here.'

Dex raked a hand through his hair. He watched her rubbing ineffectually at her neck for a moment, then walked over to sit next to her on the arm of the settee. She was surprised when he reached to rub her shoulders with firm, massaging strokes. Surprised and moved.

It was bliss for a moment, then the touch of his hands started to made her feel as if her body was on fire. It threw her senses into a deeper state of chaos.

'How's that? Do you feel better?' he asked softly.

She closed her eyes, and for a while she allowed herself to revel in the physical contact. She had been missing him so much.

'Yes…it feels really good.' Her voice was very unsteady even to her own ears.

'I understand that you've got commitments here.' He leaned his head down against hers. 'But for what it's worth our bed has felt very big and empty since you left, Alli.' The deep, husky whisper set even more flames alight inside her.

Her heart thundered in her ears. She wanted to turn in to his arms, whisper that she had missed him. But it was all a ploy; she knew him too well…he was well aware of how much he turned her on, and he wasn't above using that knowledge shamelessly if he thought it would get his baby back under his roof.

He stroked her hair back from her face and gently bent to kiss her neck. The sensitive, gentle caress was too much. She felt her defences starting to crumble.

He tipped her chin up and his lips crushed down against hers.

The passion was as vital, as intense as it had always been between them, and he tasted so good. His lips were soft, persuasive, compelling.

If she allowed this to go on she would be a complete pushover, she told herself. And when he asked her again to fly home with him she would agree without reservation.

She pulled back, her senses reeling. 'Stop it, Dex.' It took all her will-power to say those words. 'I can't cope with this right now.'

She looked up at him. His eyes were dark, hooded; it was hard to tell what was going through his mind.

She moved further away from him. 'Choose whichever bedroom you want. Both beds are made—' Whatever else she had been going to say was cut short by the baby giving a very vigorous kick. She gasped. 'Dex…!'

'What? What is it?' He knelt down beside her on the floor.

'It's OK.' She waved his concern away. 'It's just the baby kicking; he does it a lot.'

'Since when?' He met her eyes, and for a moment she could see an expression there that took her breath away even more than the boisterous movements of her unborn child.

There was a sadness there of unutterable proportions.

'He's been doing it for a while now,' she admitted. She took his hand and pressed it gently against her stomach.

After a few moments the baby struck out again.

'I felt it…my God!' Dex was totally awestruck for a moment, his hand pressing more firmly against her as the baby did it again.

Alicia jumped with the shock of it and he started to laugh. 'I think we've got ourselves a footballer!'

'You're not kidding. And it hurts!' Alicia said loudly as the baby did it again.

'Do you think he's trying to tell us something?' Dex asked with a grin.

'What? Like, Don't be so energetic out there; I'm trying to get some sleep.' She laughed.

'Or maybe he's saying, Hey, that's my dad out there. Maybe he's missed me?'

Alicia looked up at him with wide blue eyes. *She'd* missed him, she thought sadly.

'You OK?' Dex asked with a frown.

She nodded. 'He seems to have settled down.'

'Maybe we should as well.'

'Maybe.' Her heart thudded furiously hard against her chest.

She got up from the settee and started to tidy their cups back on to the tray.

'Leave that. I'll do it,' Dex offered. 'You go and turn in for the night.'

She nodded. 'Thanks. I think I will.'

She was aware of him watching her as she walked over and opened her bedroom door. She wanted to turn around and tell him it was all right if he wanted to follow her, but she didn't. It took all her will-power.

She closed the door behind her and leaned back against it. She squeezed her eyes tightly closed. If she didn't go back to Dex what would she do? She hadn't allowed herself to dwell on that up until now. She had no doubts that she would get by; she was resourceful…she wasn't frightened of being on her own. But the thought of having Dex on the sidelines of her life as a part-time father to their child was heartbreaking.

She was woken the next morning by a light tap at her bedroom door.

'Alicia, is it all right if I come in?'

'Yes.' She struggled to wake up. She had endured a dreadful night, with very little sleep. She felt exhausted.

The door opened and Dex came in carrying a cup of tea. He was fully dressed, she noticed, and her heart lurched coldly.

'Are you ready to leave?'

He nodded, and put her drink down on the bedside table.

'Thank you.' She pushed a hand self-consciously through her hair as she sat up, then watched as he went across to draw the curtains. Sunlight streamed into the bedroom.

It was a pretty room, blue, with vivid splashes of gold. Peter's photographs adorned the walls. All of them scenes of the spectacular Queensland coast.

She picked up her tea and glanced at the clock on the bedside table. It was just leaving six-thirty.

'What time have you got to be at work today?' he asked, turning back and watching her.

'Not until nine.' She sipped her drink and glanced at him over the rim of the cup. 'What time is your flight?'

'Eight o'clock.'

Silence fell between them, punctuated only by the cool whir of the air-conditioning.

'I'll come with you to the airport if you want.'

His lips twisted in a rueful smile. 'I guess I'll have to settle for that.'

He watched as she pulled the sheets back and got out of bed.

She was glad that she was wearing a pretty silk night-gown that had been designed by Rupert Williams. It cupped her breasts modestly and then fell in soft folds, minimising her pregnancy. She wondered if he was relieved that she hadn't wanted to sleep with him. She didn't suppose that pregnancy was exactly a turn-on for a man.

'I won't be long. I'll just have a quick shower.'

He nodded. 'I'll leave you to get ready, then.'

They looked at each other and she found herself remembering the time he had followed her into the shower. The feel of his hands against her naked skin, the way he had very gently and very expertly taken her to new heights of pleasure.

Of course, what she hadn't known at the time was that he was probably thinking about Maddie McDowell, a small, treacherous voice reminded her. He must have lied to her so many times about that woman.

She gave him a cool smile and walked through to the *en suite* bathroom, firmly bolting the door behind her.

It was only when she had stepped out of the shower that she realised she hadn't brought any clean clothes into the bathroom with her. She wrapped a white bath towel tightly around herself and went back out to the bedroom.

It was deserted, so she sat at her dressing table and started to blow-dry her hair.

A few moments later Dex opened the bedroom door. 'Phone call for you,' he said curtly.

'Oh!' She switched off the dryer. 'Sorry, I didn't hear it with the noise of this contraption. Who is it?'

'Peter.'

She put down the hairdryer and her brush and stood up.

Dex watched her tuck the edges of the towel more securely around her breasts before walking out into the lounge. She had incredibly long, shapely legs and the towel showed every inch of them to perfection as it finished just under the firm line of her buttocks. Her hair was almost dry, and it swung softly as she walked.

'Hi, Peter,' she said cheerfully as she lifted the receiver. 'No, you didn't wake me. I'm getting ready for work. Are you...? No, that's great.' She glanced over at Dex.

He was watching her, his dark eyes intense. He looked angry. She wondered if he was worried about the time.

'OK, well, I'll see you, then,' she told Peter hastily. 'I have to go. Dex is here.'

'Sorry about that,' she said, turning swiftly as she put the phone down. 'It won't take me a moment to get dressed.'

As she moved to go past him back into the bedroom he caught hold of her wrist.

'What is it?' Puzzled, she looked up at him.

'What did Peter want?'

'He was just warning me that he's coming to Sydney next weekend.'

'Warning you in case I'm here?'

She frowned at that. 'No. Why should it make any difference whether you're here or not?'

'I suppose I'd cramp his style,' Dex said dryly. 'He'll want you all to himself.'

'Oh, that's rubbish,' she said quickly. 'Peter isn't like that.'

'No?' Dex slanted a glance down over her body in the skimpy towel. 'I wouldn't be too sure…especially if you walk around looking like that.'

'Like what? Dex, what the hell has got into you? You know there's nothing between Peter and I.'

'Do you walk around looking like that when he's here?' His eyes burned into hers now.

'I told you last night. Peter hasn't been here since I've arrived.'

'I know what you told me.'

'Are you accusing me of lying?' She stared at him, her eyes wide. 'I've never lied to you, Dex.'

'I know. You've always been brutally bloody honest.' He glared at her. 'I'm accusing you of being a provocative little witch.'

'I…' She shook her head. 'I haven't done anything.'

'Except walk around looking gorgeous. With a "do not touch me" look in those big baby blue eyes.'

'I haven't.' She shook her head, unable to comprehend this sudden fierce mood of his.

'Haven't what? Looked gorgeous or said, Do not touch?'

'I…' She opened her mouth and didn't know how to answer that. 'You're acting crazy.'

'Yes. I'm acting crazy. That's the way you make me feel.' His hand moved and he trailed a finger over the top of her towel.

Suddenly she realised how naked she was beneath the thick cotton material. One tug and she would be standing with nothing on. That notion made her feel incredibly vulnerable, and the fact that he was wearing his suit made it even worse.

'I don't want you staying in this apartment with Peter Blake, Goddamn it.'

She frowned, anger coming to her defence. 'Don't you tell me what I can and cannot do.' She angled her head defiantly. 'I don't belong to you, Dex Rowland, or any man. I am my own person. I can do what I want, when I want. I am financially independent and—'

'And the most stubborn, irritating woman I've ever met,' he finished for her. 'You've made your point about being independent. Now I'm making my point. I need you, Alicia, and I am burning up with jealousy. The thought of you staying in this apartment with Peter is more than I can bear. I want you and my baby back home where you belong. Life is awful without you. I want you back. I want to touch you, kiss you, make love to you whenever I damn well please.'

'No, you don't.' She glared up at him. As far as she was concerned he had forfeited those rights the moment he took Maddie McDowell as his lover. 'You're a damn hypocrite, Dex Rowland. You don't want me...not really. You're just frightened somebody else might want me, because *you* want to play happy families. You'd be happy if I came back home, had the baby and then disappeared back to my career again, leaving you with our child. That's what you want.'

He stared at her. 'But that's where you're wrong, Alli. I want *you*.' As if to illustrate his point, his hands moved up under the towel in a firm, possessive way. 'I want you right now.'

'Don't do that.' Her heart skidded crazily. In the scuffle to take his hands away her towel slipped. Her breasts were pressed against the smooth dark suit.

'You've no idea how much I want you.' He bent his head and kissed her naked shoulder, his voice husky with longing.

She took a deep, shuddering breath and tried to force herself to tell him to stop. But now she didn't want him to stop. Her anger had changed to need.

He kissed her shoulders again, then the sides of her neck, then her ears.

She groaned. Dex had always been a master at finding all the little areas that turned her on.

She felt herself pressed back against the wall. Her hands clung to him as his head lowered and he kissed the pulse-point at the base of her throat. Then the hollow between her breasts.

He took hold of her hands and she let go of the towel without contention. Her body was pressed so close against his that it didn't fall.

Her palms pressed back against the coolness of the wall as his lips grazed the sensitive curves of her breast. She was so aroused that she couldn't remember what they had been arguing about…what had caused her to lose her temper. All she knew was here and now, and that this was the man she loved with all her heart.

Then suddenly he was moving back from her. She had to grab the towel before it fell to the floor. She held it in front of her and stared up at him wordlessly, wondering why he had stopped.

'I'm sorry, Alli.' He shook his head and backed away from her. 'I shouldn't have started this…I'm really sorry.'

He raked a hand through the darkness of his hair in a gesture of utter remorse. Then he turned away from her to pick up his flight bag which he had left beside the door.

She took the opportunity to secure the towel around her body. 'Dex, I—'

'Look, don't say anything. You were right and I was wrong. I'm sorry. I should never have talked you into getting married and it's absurd of me to try and tell you what to do.'

He paused, his hand on the door handle. 'It's best that I just leave.'

Her heart felt as if it were ready to break in two. Even if she had known what to say she wouldn't have had the strength to say it.

'If you want to come back to Queensland, Alicia, I won't bother you. In fact I'll move out of the house and you can have it. How's that?'

Still she said nothing. Her breathing was too raw, too ragged.

'You think about what you want,' he said quietly. 'I know you want to be independent, but bear in mind that I'd like to provide well for you and the baby.'

Her eyes glistened with tears.

'I hope you'll find it in your heart to forgive me,' he said quietly. 'The problem is that I love you, Alli. I always have and I always will, and it's making me crazy.'

For a second she wondered if she had misheard. She had longed to hear those words for so long that she couldn't believe they were falling from his lips now.

By the time she had rallied her thoughts sufficiently to answer, the door had closed behind him. She ran to open it but he had gone. Only the light on the lift told her that he was on his way downstairs.

She stood in the doorway, agitated and frustrated. But for her state of undress she would have run after him.

She slammed the door shut and leaned back against it. Did Dex really love her, or was this some cruel ruse to make her go back to him? She hardly dared to believe what he had just told her.

It had to be his way of getting her back, she decided forcefully. She wouldn't get her hopes up; she wouldn't believe him.

The phone rang and she went across to answer it.

It was Peter. 'Did you say Dex was there?' he asked cautiously.

'Yes, I did. But you're all right; he's gone now.' Alicia tried to sound cheerful.

'Are you OK?'

'I think so.' She took a deep breath. 'When did you say you were coming down to Sydney?'

'Next weekend. Why?'

'I might not be here,' Alicia decided suddenly. 'We might be on planes that pass in the night.' She tried to make a joke of it. 'I'm going to see if I can get a flight home. In fact I'm going to try and get home today; I need to talk to Dex.'

'Don't forget you're supposed to be doing a fashion shoot for Rupert today. You can't just leave,' Peter cautioned.

Alicia bit down on her lip. He was right. She had obligations here, and the first of those was another modelling session this morning.

'But, Alicia, I don't want to interfere. If you want to go to Dex, maybe you should—'

'No.' She cut across him firmly. 'You're right. I have obligations here.'

CHAPTER THIRTEEN

DEX couldn't find anything in the office. He had given Vicky the day off and now he was regretting it.

He swore under his breath and slammed the filing cabinets shut.

He went to Alicia's desk and pulled open some of the drawers.

If the list was there he couldn't see it. All he could see was a pair of baby's booties. He picked them up. They were so tiny and cute that for a moment he could only stare at the yellow knitted garments and feel pain. He had never known pain like it.

He put them back where he had found them and slammed the drawer closed.

Maybe he shouldn't have come straight from the airport to the office. He was tired, and there wasn't anything here that couldn't wait until tomorrow.

He reached to pick up the post. It was mostly the usual junk mail. He skipped through it without interest, and then came across an envelope with what looked like Alicia's handwriting on it.

Impatiently he tore it open. It was a birthday card: 'Happy Birthday to My Husband love always, Alicia.

He stared at it. Of course it meant nothing. People wrote things like that without even thinking about the words. It didn't mean a thing.

She had probably sent it to the office because she knew he opened his business mail first thing every morning and the post at home waited until the evening. She was always so organised. But her plans had gone astray, because on his birthday he hadn't come to work. Instead he had flown to see her.

He read the card again, and then pushed it back in the envelope. 'Love always' didn't mean anything. She had made it clear often enough that she didn't love him. Except perhaps once on their honeymoon, when she had tried to be kind, had joked and made it seem as if she was falling seriously for him. But of course she hadn't been...it was just Alicia's way. She was kind-hearted, sweet...when she wasn't being bloody awkward. He scowled at the envelope and pushed it back with the junk mail.

Hell, what an eventful few months it had been. Married, separated, a child on the way. And a partner who had driven him demented. Maddie was truly unhinged. Although she had been crafty enough to wait until their contract was signed before starting to make a nuisance of herself.

He thought about the way she had thrown herself at him in Perth, and then again on the day of his wedding. It had been at that moment that he had realised how much he loved Alli...how much he really wanted to make a commitment to her for life and forsake all others.

Since Clare he hadn't thought he would feel like that again. It was ironic that the one woman he wanted with all his heart should totally reject him.

He'd have to chalk it up to experience. He slammed the post into a drawer and shut it. Then wondered again where that damn list had gone. If he hadn't got rid of Maddie he would have wondered if she had taken it. He had no doubt in his mind that she had taken the list that they'd thought Alli had lost. The more he'd thought over that incident later, the more he'd been convinced of it. That woman was crazy—anyway, he was well rid of her now.

He opened another drawer in desperation. There was nothing in there except a few papers and a bottle of Alicia's perfume. He brought it out and sprayed a little of it on the air. It was light and delicately feminine. If he leaned his head back against the chair and breathed in he could almost imagine that Alli was here now. That she was with him.

God, he knew no rest, no peace of mind anywhere, he thought with fury. At home he found reminders of his wife everywhere. From her toothpaste and her favourite soap in the bathroom to the kitchen cupboards and that damned herbal tea she liked to drink.

How moronic could a guy get? he mocked himself. When you felt saddened by the sight of a packet of cam-omile tea it was time to wrap up.

He squeezed his eyes tightly closed and tried to think where that list was. He wouldn't give Alicia another thought...not one.

It was starting to go dark when Alicia stepped out of Cairns Airport and hailed a taxi to take her home.

The sky was a ruby-red, the palm trees and mountains dark silhouettes against the flame sky.

The taxi driver kept up a constant chatter as they sped along the Cook Highway. Alicia was glad of the distraction from her own thoughts.

It was only when he turned the taxi down the lane that led to their house that her mind wandered away from the trivial conversation.

The lights in the lounge were on; golden welcoming light spilled out on to the deck.

She felt her heart beating faster as the taxi pulled to a halt. She looked up towards the front door, almost expect-ing it to open and Dex to come out. It remained firmly closed.

'I'll give you a hand with your bags up the steps,' the taxi driver said cheerfully.

'Thanks.' She stepped out into the warmth of the eve-ning. There was a stiff breeze stirring the gum trees, and the waves were pounding in against the shore just below them.

As the taxi drove away down the dark winding road Alicia found her front door key and stepped into the house.

The lounge was deserted, though all the lights were on and the radio was loudly blaring out the day's news.

It felt good to be home. She looked around at the familiar furnishings, the embroidered cushions, the pictures of her wedding on the mantelpiece.

She hoped to high heaven that Dex had meant those parting words yesterday. That he loved her, that he missed her. On the strength of them she had given up everything in Sydney. On the strength of them she didn't care about ever going back. This was where she belonged.

'Hello?' Her voice was unnaturally shaky as she called out. She felt nervous suddenly.

There was no reply. She put her suitcase down and walked through to the kitchen.

Vicky was in there, making coffee. She nearly dropped her cup as she turned and saw Alicia.

'What are you doing here?' she gasped in surprise, putting down the drink and coming to embrace her.

'Couldn't stay away a moment longer.' Alicia grinned. 'Thought I'd better get back and make sure you return to school.'

'I'm looking forward to it,' Vicky replied. 'After working for Dex these last few weeks I know what hard work is.'

'I thought you'd enjoyed it?'

'I did. But we've had one or two problems.'

'You didn't mention them to me on the phone.'

'Dex handled them.' Vicky shrugged. 'They were mostly to do with Maddie McDowell. The moment you left she was never away from the office. Even turned up here late one night. She seemed to have a major fixation on Dex.'

'Oh?' Alicia could feel her heart racing at double speed.

'He got rid of her. Broke their contract. I've never seen him so angry.'

'Broke the contract?' Alicia was stunned. 'That will have cost fortunes.'

Vicky nodded. 'It was touch and go whether the whole business was going to go under. That was why Dex didn't want me to tell you. He didn't want you to worry. Anyway it's all sorted out now. He's struck a deal with a company called Banks. We heard from them today and they're prepared to pay Maddie off and sort the legal fees.'

'So the business is OK?'

'More than just OK. Dex has done a really clever deal. I don't understand him; he should be on top of the world and yet he's thoroughly miserable.'

'Where is he?'

'He went back to the office after dinner. He'll be surprised to see you.' She frowned. 'Why didn't you come home with him yesterday?'

'I had one last modelling job to do.' Alicia picked her car keys up from the hook behind the door. 'I'm going to go and surprise him.'

Vicky grinned. 'I'd like to see the look on his face when he sees you.'

Alicia's car was parked in the garage. She had difficulty getting it started, and even when she did it coughed and spluttered as she turned it up the lane towards the main road.

She wondered if this was such a good idea. Maybe it would have been better to wait for Dex to return.

The windscreen was filthy, so she sprayed it with water and turned on the wipers. It seemed to make the problem worse; she could hardly see out now.

She wondered if there was an old cloth on the floor that she could wipe it with. She'd always used to have one.

Quickly she turned on the light inside the car and looked down towards the floor.

She didn't see a cloth. What she did see was a long brown snake, uncoiling from the floor and sliding up the passenger seat.

The shock held her paralysed for a second. She could see the forked tongue flicking out, the scaly skin shiny in the overhead light.

She looked back towards the road and too late noticed that her car had veered from her side of the road and that there was a car heading straight for her. It all seemed to happen in slow motion. She heard the blare of a horn as she swerved to avoid the oncoming vehicle, and although she hadn't been travelling fast she lost control of her car and it skidded from the road down into the ditch. The last thing she remembered was her head hitting the side window with a vicious crack, then everything went black.

'Alicia.' The voice seemed to be coming from a great distance. 'Alicia, are you all right?'

It sounded like Dex. She tried to open her eyes but she couldn't. It was the strangest sensation and it scared her.

She could hear the creak of the driver's door being wrenched open and she felt herself being caught in strong arms and lifted gently.

There was a smell of burning rubber; it made her feel sick. She groaned and buried her head against the softness of a silk shirt. Now she could smell the familiar scent of Dex's cologne. The feeling of sickness passed. Her head was thumping as if people with hammers were at work inside her.

'Alicia, are you all right?'

She could feel his hands moving over her body, as if checking for broken bones. She remembered the snake, the forked tongue, and in her mind she saw it pouncing on her, sinking fangs into the soft flesh of her upper arm. She shuddered, and then couldn't stop shaking.

'Alicia, please be all right. If anything should happen to you...' The anguish in Dex's voice was the last thing she heard.

Her head was resting against something soft. She opened her eyes. The room swam in front of her, as if it was enveloped in a heat haze. She couldn't focus on anything clearly. She saw a dark shadow next to her bed, the brightness of a window. Nothing made any sense. She felt dehydrated; her mouth was rough and sore.

She needed a drink, but she couldn't find her voice to ask for one.

Where was she? she wondered, feeling panicky. Where was Dex?

'She's coming round.' The whispered voice wasn't familiar.

She closed her eyes again, feeling exhausted. Then someone was holding something to her lips. She felt the wet trickle of water and sipped it thankfully.

'Darling? Alicia?' The husky concern of her husband's voice brought tears to her eyes. She opened them again.

The dark shadow next to her was taking shape.

She felt a hand stroking the side of her face.

'Where am I?' she whispered as his face came suddenly into focus.

'Hospital. But you're going to be fine.' The gentle, reassuring voice was at odds with the way he looked. His skin was pale, his eyes dark with anguish.

She frowned. 'You look ill. Are you feeling all right?'

For a moment he smiled, and it banished the bleakness from his eyes. 'I've just been so worried about you. You gave me a terrible scare.'

'Did I?' She frowned. She couldn't remember why she

had scared him. She felt weird. As if she wasn't in her own body. As if she had woken up into some kind of dream.

She looked around. They were alone in a private room, the walls were white, the bedcovers were white. Dex stood out starkly with his dark hair and dark clothes.

'You had an accident in the car, remember?' he said gently. 'You nearly ran straight into me.'

Her heart missed a beat as suddenly she saw the scene again. The snake, the car, the crack of her head.

She groaned. 'What about the baby? Is my baby all right?' She felt her voice rising, strong with anguish, when he didn't answer her. 'Dex, tell me the truth.' Her voice was a command, and she ran her hand down towards her stomach, panic tearing her apart.

'Stop it, Alli.' He caught hold of her hand and held it. 'They've done tests…and as far as they can tell everything is fine with the baby.'

'What do you mean, as far as they can tell?' Her eyes were wide blue oceans in the smallness of her face.

'Just what I said. They haven't come back yet with the rest of the results.'

She stared at him, absolutely stricken.

'It will be all right, Alli,' he said, squeezing her hand gently.

'But what if it isn't?' Tears were rolling down the coolness of her cheeks in silent witness of the horror of this situation.

'It will.' His voice was firm. He wiped her tears away with his fingers. 'Come on, sweetheart, you've got to be strong. I want you to get well. That's the most important thing in the world to me.'

She shook her head and bit down on her lip. 'Your baby is the most important thing in the world to you, and if I lose it…' Her voice caught and refused to continue. Her mind was racing. Her body felt so sore suddenly, as if she had been run over by a tank. Her head was pounding. 'If I lose it you won't want me any more.'

She saw the shock in his eyes. 'Darling, that's just not true…I love you with all my heart and I'll always want you, no matter what.'

'Really?' Her voice was trembling and unsure.

He nodded. 'The baby will be fine…' He hesitated, his eyes darkening. 'And if it's not we'll face that together.'

She pulled her hand away from his and touched the blankets that covered her stomach. She remembered how vigorously the baby had been kicking only yesterday, and the salt of her tears ran over the softness of her lips. 'I can't bear it Dex… If the baby is…is dead… I couldn't bear it.'

She tried to sit up, but he caught hold of her, pulling her in against his shoulder. She clung to him, listening to the sound of his heart beating, trying to gather her strength and face whatever had to be faced.

'It's in God's hands, Alli.' Dex whispered against her ear. 'And whatever happens, know that I love you.'

'I love you too,' she whispered through her tears. He pulled back from her and they looked at each other for long moments.

'Do you know how much I've longed to hear you say those words?' he whispered.

'I've said them before—'

He shook his head. 'Not and meant them. Marriage to me was second-best to the career you longed for. I've always known that.'

'Dex, that's just not true,' she whispered softly. 'My love for you has always come first.'

He frowned, as if he just couldn't believe her. 'So why did you go away?'

'Because I found out about your affair with Maddie. How you'd lied about it being over. I just couldn't stand it.' She wiped her tears away from her face and lay back against her pillow. 'It is over now, isn't it, Dex?'

Dex stared at her. 'Alli, I've never lied to you. The affair was over years ago.'

'That's not true. I heard you together…I saw you.' She reached for the glass of water that sat by her bed. Her hand wasn't steady and he reached to help her.

'Saw and heard what?' Dex sounded genuinely perplexed.

'Both of you—at that party.' Alicia tried not to sound as furious and as hurt as she felt, but her hand betrayed her by trembling so much that she had to put the glass of water back down on the table beside her.

'You were alone in her office. Don't try to tell me that it was all business. You looked too involved for that. You said you needed her. She reminded you that you didn't love me…' Her voice choked with the pain of that memory. 'That you couldn't even say the words.'

'When I said I needed her I was talking about business, and the fact that she had backed me financially.' Dex bit down on his lip. 'Darling, obviously you didn't hang around to listen any further, because I *did* tell her just how much I love you, how much I want our child. But she was…weird. That's the only word I can use to explain her. It was as if she'd only hear what she wanted to hear and then she'd twist the truth.' He shrugged. 'I've been cursing myself since I signed the contract with her in Perth. She is slightly mad, I think. You know she even came to my apartment on the day of our wedding? I didn't tell you that before because you were so upset about the damn card she slipped into my bag. And I wasn't sure if you would believe me that nothing happened. She flung herself at me. I was never so glad to see Peter at the door.'

'Oh, Dex! I've been so frightened that you really wanted

her. I kept thinking that maybe she reminded you of Clare and that was why you were attracted to her.'

'Hell, no!' Dex looked appalled.

'As I was leaving her party she told me that you were having an affair. She told me that if I confronted you she would make sure you lost your business. That she would withdraw her money and ruin you.'

Dex swore under his breath. 'That sounds about par for the course,' he said grimly. 'She kept reminding me that we had a business agreement and that I needed her. But when it boiled right down to it she needed me more than I needed her. I had the know-how and the product; she only ever had the money. In the end it was better just to blow her out altogether and take my chances elsewhere. I didn't tell you that I was still having problems with her because I didn't want to worry you.' He stroked her hair back from her face. 'The whole thing was a nightmare, but I've never lied to you, darling.'

'Some guy at the party thought Maddie was your wife— said he'd seen you out together and you'd introduced her as your partner—'

'*Business* partner,' Dex corrected firmly. 'That was the evening Maddie and I had a coffee together while I tried to talk some sense into her…I was fighting a losing battle.'

'Oh, Dex, I've allowed her to mess up our lives so much.' Her eyes shimmered with tears.

He stroked the salt wetness from her cheeks. 'Everything's going to be all right now. She's out of our lives.' He reached across and kissed her; he could taste the salt of her tears on his lips, feel the heat of her love. He closed his eyes and held her tight.

'I've been so damned miserable without you,' he whispered.

'Me too.' Her voice was very unsteady as she fought not to cry again.

For a while they just held each other without saying anything, getting strength from each other. 'Do you think the
baby will be all right?' Alicia whispered. 'When did they
say they'd have the test results?'

'They didn't.' His voice was grim. 'I've been out several
times to talk to the doctor.'

Alicia took a deep breath. She didn't dare contemplate
the worst. 'Were you really in the car that I swerved to
avoid?' she asked shakily.

'Yes. What happened anyway? You veered completely
over to the wrong side of the road.'

'There was a snake in the car.'

'A snake!'

She nodded. 'I switched on the car light to find a cloth
to wipe the windscreen and there it was, sliding up the
passenger seat.' She shuddered at the memory. 'The next
moment I'd lost control of the car.'

'Good job neither of us were driving fast.' His voice was
rough with emotion. 'You really frightened me, Alli.'

'I was pretty scared myself.' Then, after a moment, she
whispered, 'I still am. Where is that doctor, Dex? I don't
think I can stand this much longer.'

He pulled away from her. 'I'll go and see what I can
find out.' He was in the process of rising from his chair
when the doctor came into the room. He was a young man
in his twenties, with a friendly, reassuring air about him.

'The nurse said you'd come round.' He smiled at her.
'How are you feeling?'

'I'd feel better if you told me that my baby is all right.'
She looked up at him with wide, anxious eyes and he
smiled.

'Everything is fine. I've just had the last of the test results
and you have a perfectly healthy child. There's no reason
why you shouldn't have a completely normal and good
delivery in a few months' time.'

Alicia's eyes glistened with tears of joy and Dex squeezed her hand.

'Everything is going to be all right,' he whispered softly. 'We've had a very close call, Alli.'

She nodded, knowing that he was talking about more than the accident.

The doctor came closer to check her over, shine a light in her eyes, take her pulse. Then he nodded, as if satisfied. 'How does your head feel?'

'As if I'd been to one almighty party last night.'

He smiled at that.

'It should wear off as the day goes on. We'll keep you in for another few hours' observation, just to be on the safe side. Then your husband can take you home.'

Alicia smiled over at Dex. 'That sounds like heaven,' she said gently.

'Sure does.' He smiled back at her.

At some point the doctor must have left the room, because when Alicia pulled her eyes away from Dex he was gone.

Dex got to his feet. 'I better go ring Vicky. She stayed over at Jenny's last night but I'm sure she didn't get a wink of sleep. She's been worried sick about you.'

'OK.' Alicia smiled. 'But first tell me you love me just one more time.'

'I'll tell you that as many times as you want.' He smiled and came to sit on the side of her bed. Her arms wound up around his neck and gently he kissed her.

'I'm sorry I didn't believe you about Maddie—'

'I blame myself.' Dex cut across her. 'I should have confided in you more, told you everything.' His eyes moved over her face with such love that it took her breath away. 'I'm sorry, Alicia; I underestimated you. It's only recently that I've grown to realise just how much strength of spirit lies under that exterior of soft, vulnerable femininity. I wanted to be the strong hero who made everything right so that you'd never have to worry again. I know how awful your childhood was, and I just wanted to make everything perfect for you. It was very condescending of me, I realise that now, especially in the light of you going off to Sydney and proving that you don't need me at all.'

'But I do need you, Dex,' she whispered softly. 'I'd never have gone off to Sydney if I'd thought that you felt so deeply about me. It was only the knowledge that you didn't love me that drove me away.'

He reached and kissed her with tender passion. 'Darling, you mean the whole world to me,' he whispered. 'I've been out of my mind since you left. I was even jealous of Peter—'

'There is no romance between Peter and I,' Alicia put in quickly. 'You're not going to fall out with him, are you, Dex? He's been a good friend to me—'

'No, Alli, I hold no animosity towards Peter. Not now I've got you back. Hopefully we've all learnt from our mistakes…I know I have. I'll never let you go again.'

CHAPTER FOURTEEN

DEX closed the filing cabinet and went to sit behind his desk. He glanced at his watch. It was nearly time to pack up. He was taking Alicia for dinner.

He glanced at the new designs on his desk and felt a glimmer of excitement at how the business had taken off. Maybe he would just do a couple more minutes. Make a few phone calls.

He searched on the desk for a letter that he'd been reading earlier and couldn't find it.

The door to his office opened and Alicia came in.

The sight of her, as always, made his heart beat faster, made the day seem brighter. She looked gorgeous: her long blonde hair gleaming, her complexion creamy, her eyes wide and inviting. She was wearing a soft vanilla suit that looked stylish and cool. She was in the last weeks of pregnancy now, and he didn't think she had ever looked as radiant, as desirable.

'You're not going to be much longer, are you?' she asked gently. 'Remember we're meeting Vicky and Robbie for dinner.'

'I haven't forgotten,' Dex assured her. 'Have you seen that letter Josh sent me?' he asked her distractedly.

'Second drawer down, third file in.' She grinned.

He opened the drawer, and sure enough the letter was in the file. 'You're unbelievable sometimes,' he declared.

'When you become a multi-millionaire will you still want me for your secretary?' she asked softly.

'Will you still want to be my secretary?' The dark eyes were serious and intent.

They stared at each other silently for a moment.

'Depends on the working conditions.' She grinned again. 'And just how filthy rich you get.'

He laughed. 'I love it when you talk dirty.'

He reached out and took hold of her hand, pulling her around the desk. 'Alicia, I love you,' he groaned.

'Well, I *am* a damn good secretary.'

'Damn good at everything,' he murmured as she settled herself on his lap. 'That's your problem.'

'I wasn't aware that I had one…'

He kissed her, and it was long moments before either spoke again.

A sudden commotion in the other room made them pull apart.

Through the open doorway they watched their son as he hurtled around the room, playing with a small plane held high above his head.

'I think he's trying to tell us he's ready to go for dinner now,' Alicia said with a smile.

'I think you're right… Sam, come here,' Dex called out, and the child came racing in through the door at an unsteady full speed to launch himself straight at them with a sunny smile.

He was just three, and the image of his father. Same dark hair and dark eyes, same bundle of mischief, Alicia thought, with a swell of love in her heart.

She stood up, and Dex switched off his computer before swinging the child up into his arms.

Together they left the house. It was a clear, sunny afternoon and the swimming pool sparkled invitingly. Dex unlocked his Jaguar and strapped Sam into the child seat at the back, then they set off down the long winding drive, just stopping to wait for the electric gates to open.

Alicia rested her hand over her stomach.

'Is he kicking again?' Dex asked with a grin.

'There's some movement all right,' she answered with a smile. 'But this time I think I'm going to have a little girl.'

'Katy.' Dex looked across at her with love and tenderness.

'Katy,' she agreed, and smiled.

In the rearview mirror Dex could see their house, a sprawling, impressive mansion. But it was nothing to the riches that surrounded him in this car.

He reached across and took his wife's hand in his for just a moment.

He was a lucky man.

MILLS & BOON®

Makes
any time
special

Enjoy a romantic novel from
Mills & Boon®

Presents™ Enchanted™ Temptation

Historical Romance™ Medical Romance™

MILLS & BOON®

Next Month's Romance Titles

♡

Each month you can choose from a wide variety of romance novels from Mills & Boon®. Below are the new titles to look out for next month from the Presents...™ and Enchanted™ series.

Presents...™

A CONVENIENT BRIDEGROOM	Helen Bianchin
IRRESISTIBLE TEMPTATION	Sara Craven
THE BAD GIRL BRIDE	Jennifer Drew
MISTRESS FOR A NIGHT	Diana Hamilton
A TREACHEROUS SEDUCTION	Penny Jordan
ACCIDENTAL BABY	Kim Lawrence
THE BABY GAMBIT	Anne Mather
A MAN TO MARRY	Carole Mortimer

Enchanted™

KIDS INCLUDED!	Caroline Anderson
PARENTS WANTED!	Ruth Jean Dale
MAKING MR RIGHT	Val Daniels
A VERY PRIVATE MAN	Jane Donnelly
LAST-MINUTE BRIDEGROOM	Linda Miles
DR. DAD	Julianna Morris
DISCOVERING DAISY	Betty Neels
UNDERCOVER BACHELOR	Rebecca Winters

On sale from 6th August 1999

H1 9907

Available at most branches of WH Smith, Tesco, Asda, Martins, Borders, Easons, Volume One/James Thin and most good paperback bookshops

THE Regency COLLECTION

Where rogues find romance

Look out for the fourth volume in this limited collection of Regency Romances from Mills & Boon® in August.

Featuring:

The Outrageous Dowager
by Sarah Westleigh

and

Devil-May-Dare
by Mary Nichols

Still only £4.99

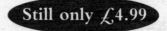

MILLS & BOON®
Makes any time special™

Available at most branches of WH Smith, Tesco, Martins, Borders, Easons, Volume One/James Thin and most good paperback bookshops

4 FREE
books and a surprise gift!

We would like to take this opportunity to thank you for reading this Mills & Boon® book by offering you the chance to take FOUR more specially selected titles from the Presents…™ series absolutely FREE! We're also making this offer to introduce you to the benefits of the Reader Service™—

- ★ FREE home delivery
- ★ FREE gifts and competitions
- ★ FREE monthly Newsletter
- ★ Exclusive Reader Service discounts
- ★ Books available before they're in the shops

Accepting these FREE books and gift places you under no obligation to buy, you may cancel at any time, even after receiving your free shipment. Simply complete your details below and return the entire page to the address below. *You don't even need a stamp!*

YES! Please send me 4 free Presents… books and a surprise gift. I understand that unless you hear from me, I will receive 6 superb new titles every month for just £2.40 each, postage and packing free. I am under no obligation to purchase any books and may cancel my subscription at any time. The free books and gift will be mine to keep in any case.

P9EA

Ms/Mrs/Miss/Mr ....Initials................................
BLOCK CAPITALS PLEASE

Surname ....

Address ....

....

....Postcode..............................

Send this whole page to:
THE READER SERVICE, FREEPOST CN81, CROYDON, CR9 3WZ
(Eire readers please send coupon to: P.O. BOX 4546, DUBLIN 24.)

MILLS & BOON®

London streets aren't just paved with gold— they're home to three of the world's most eligible bachelors!

NOTTING HILL GROOMS

Three popular Presents…™ authors bring you the **Notting Hill Grooms**—three eligible bachelors each looking for a wife.

SARA CRAVEN
Irresistible Temptation
published August 1999

MARY LYONS
Reform of the Playboy
published September 1999

SOPHIE WESTON
The Millionaire Affair
published October 1999